MATCHED WITH HER ATHLETE BOSS

ROMANCE BY LOVE, AUSTEN

BRITNEY M. MILLS

1

KENZIE

Cleaning Enthusiast is my middle name. Or at least it should be.

My roommates would agree that this title fits. Aside from hiding chocolate bars in random places around the house for emergencies, I like to keep things in order. I went down an internet rabbit-hole a few days ago, surprised by how much can go into the psychology of cleaning.

I did a spring cleaning on the house back in April and now, mid-way through July, I'm starting over again. There's nothing wrong with a cleaning overhaul every three months, right? And not just the deep clean kind. My brother let me use his truck to take a bunch of bags to a donation center from all of the Spice House roomies.

Growing up as the only daughter of Brian Sullivan and Felicia Tomlinson, with a slew of half-brothers, my life has been an adventure for sure.

So, as of six days ago, I started an organizing business. Do I have clients yet? No. But I've got business cards and that's the true start of being an entrepreneur, right?

How does a girl who can't keep a job claim to be an expert in organizing a space?

But the overriding issue in holding down a job is that if it's boring or they don't keep things clean, I have a hard time focusing on anything but the mess.

Because my dad is a hoarder at home but the epitome of neat and tidy when it comes to the ice rink he manages. How he can manage both makes me wonder if it's a superpower, like Superman and Clark Kent.

The hoarding increased over my middle school and high school years. His need to keep everything caused so many fights between my mother and father at the beginning of their marriage that while there were still other things wrong, I think it eventually led to their divorce.

Mom is on marriage number four and Dad has a girlfriend, last time I heard.

Their relationships alone should've been a key indicator for how my love life would go. No, I've never been married, but I was close once. The breakup was devastating at first, but looking back, I call it a blessing. Other than that, I usually go on a few dates with men—not at the same time of course—land then end up sliding into the friend zone.

I wish I didn't understand why. Guys want a woman who's sexy and coy, not someone like me who slinks around in workout clothes or sweatpants every chance I can.

It's the by-product of growing up a tom-boy. I love anything to do with sports, or things that are high adrenaline. And my competition level is off the charts. Chances are high I'm not letting a man win just to save his ego.

And after my last relationship with Johnny where he slowly ghosted me, then magically reappeared three months later to ask for advice on what to do with this new girl he liked, I might as well start an advice column for guys. It would be called *Girl Talk* or something like that.

Does every one of these guys break my heart? No, but the one that hurt the worst left me for a woman with the title of Princess.

There is a unicorn, the one guy I can never have because I'm not at all like the models he has on his arm at all the big fancy events he's invited to. If there was a Guinness Record for longest crush, it would probably have my name in there soon when it comes to Treydon Hatch, Boston Breeze center who should be the right wing.

At least I'm trying to cure myself of that. It's nice to think about someone I don't actually know, well aside from meeting him after one of his games a few weeks ago. There are no attachment issues, or wondering where the relationship will go in a few weeks. I'm the fan girl.

I straighten my shoulders and smile. That's why I'm going solo, a lot like that song that was popular a few years ago. I'm not going to worry about guys and I'm done dating.

My biggest problem right now is telling Dad that I'm going to be my own boss. I called my mom last night, mostly because she's living in Europe and I needed something to talk about with her.

I can still hear her voice saying, "MacKenzie, that sounds like a lot of work." The woman was laying out in the sun at a private resort her newest husband owns. I'm not good at sitting still for that long.

A banking alert pops up on my phone. Three dollars and fifty-seven cents are all that's in my checking account right now. I still have to pick up my last check from the ABC You Better Drugstore, but that will go toward gas and food.

And now I'm wondering if starting my own business is a bad idea. That seems to be the common thread in my life lately. Excited to doubting every little thing.

The Kenzie from thirty minutes ago thought the plan was solid, excited to hold the business cards she designed. Now

I'm thinking this dream might not get me through the month.

I take a deep breath before entering the rink my father manages. He's been at the Alvey Ice Arena for nearly three decades and some of my favorite memories are from the ice and the people, the smell of burnt popcorn and stinky skates. I know those aren't the typical details normal people would give to remember a place fondly, but as an awkward teen, I thought I could take over the world when inside its walls.

Starting a new business isn't something I've had on one of my many lists, but after going through jobs like a pack of Double Stuf Oreos, maybe it's time to become an entrepreneur.

"You've got this, Kenz," I whisper to myself. "You've got a lot of experience and can make a difference in people's lives. Or at least their sanity level."

Doubt creeps in that people will actually pay for someone to organize their home. I'm also nervous my dad won't get behind it. He loved telling people I worked in marketing, but that was six jobs and nine months ago now.

This twenty-five-year-old ex-collegiate athlete still can't figure out what to do with her life. A career, a relationship, whether or not I should accept the newest diet plan into my regime. I've checked the undecided box on all those big decisions. My parents try to guide me in all the areas of my life, but either I'm stubborn or I have perpetual bad luck. Honestly, I'm leaning toward the second one.

Teenage me would definitely be jealous that I got to meet Trey Hatch now that he's a professional hockey star. At this point, though, I don't have the luxury of worrying about men.

I'd like to have enough money to eat in the coming weeks.

"Hey Mac, will you restock the gear that just came in?" my dad asks when I walk into the hockey shop near the entrance to the rink. He's carrying a large crate of cleaning supplies to wipe up the counter and keep things in top shape here at the rink.

Which is interesting because he doesn't have the same standards at home.

"Dad," I say, glancing around. "Remember, I go by Kenzie now."

He waves a hand in the air. "Old habits die hard. I'll try to remember, but I don't know why you wanted to change your name, anyway."

It's the same old conversation. Once I got to college, I found it the perfect opportunity to reinvent myself. I'd dropped some pounds through the summer before my freshman year thanks to the grueling workout schedule and diet plan my college hockey coach had sent me. I'd gotten the braces off (yes, way too late) and contacts were more practical than the thick glasses I sported for nearly a decade at that point.

It was like my own *Ugly Duckling* makeover story.

"You named me Mackenzie, Dad. I'm still using part of that name."

He scrunches his nose a bit and nods. "I know, but it doesn't match you as well. Mac-Attack is catchy when you're on the ice."

"There are names that rhyme with Kenzie," I say. When he opens his mouth to challenge me, I say, "But I'm not coming up with any good ones at the moment."

He laughs as he uses a box cutter to slice through the tape on the top of the boxes. I walk over, grateful for the distraction from the well of self-pity I'd started spiraling into. Restocking is my favorite job. Seeing all the shiny new hockey gear hanging on the walls of the small hockey shop has always been a rush. Nerd status unlocked over here.

Dad wipes down the counter next to me. "What's new in your life? I thought you were working at the drugstore."

Shaking my head, I open the bag of pucks, dumping them into the large bin. "Nope. My co-worker, Betty, lost it a few days ago when the manager declined her request for a raise. She knocked down every item in four aisles before the cops came and took her away."

My dad glances up, and I know his mind is turning this information over. "What does that have to do with you?"

I blow out a breath. Even though I feel justified in quitting, I've done something similar to the last ten jobs I've had. Find something small and then give my notice.

"I asked if the manager was going to help in the cleanup or bring in some other help to get the store ready for customers. He said no." I pause, trying not to relive every moment with exact clarity. "I told him I was done."

A soft smile forms on my dad's face and he shakes his head. He focuses on adjusting some of the pegs that hold up the equipment, which means he's trying to decide how to handle the situation.

"You know I love having you here, Ma–Kenz, but you need a plan for your life. I don't know how you could keep things around the house so clean but struggle with something like holding down a job."

"I do have a plan," I say, my defenses rising.

He tilts his head to the side and purses his lips, letting me know he doesn't believe that for one second.

"Someday I want to work for the Boston Breeze. Even if I'm the one who has to sit behind the goal and press the buzzer to let the ref know the puck went in, I'd be happy."

Dad laughs at that. "You've been saying the same thing for fifteen years, pumpkin. Have you applied to work for their organization?"

I nod, biting back the frustration of another rejection email I'd received this morning. It was a pipe dream to work with the Breeze organization, but I'm not one to give up on things that mean a lot to me. "I've just got to keep trying."

"Okay, what about in the meantime? How are you going to

afford rent and the other living expenses? I know it's not cheap, especially where you live."

Gulp.

I hesitate, not sure if I'm ready to share my plans. I like to have things perfect before I share. I learned to have a thick skin with my hockey skills, doing my best to listen to coaches and put it into practice, but having something I have a passion for shot down because of how "hard it will be" to get things started isn't something I'm ready to hear.

Blowing out a deep breath, I say, "I'm starting an organizational business. I'd come in and help people figure out where to put things and get their life in order. Right now, I'll take any mess that needs to be cleaned up."

Dad goes silent for several moments, and my stomach is in knots. Usually, I can read him like my favorite cozy mystery books, but he's got everything on lock down. Finally, he nods, pausing his cleaning. "You're really good at that. I know we would've drowned at the house if you weren't constantly keeping things reined in while you lived there."

We laugh, both of us remembering all the fights we'd had growing up. When your father is a hoarder, debates about what to keep and what to chuck are a daily occurrence. Most of the time, I'd have to hide whatever I was throwing out and put it in a dumpster a few blocks away so it wouldn't magically reappear in the house.

"You always kept things interesting. Like bringing home that bike someone had made of pop cans."

We both laugh louder. "You sat on it and the whole thing folded in on itself."

"I was five. What was I supposed to think? I didn't know you'd meant it as a decoration for our front yard. I mean, it wasn't following your typical aesthetic."

"True. Everything else was rusted out."

I grin as I think of the quirks of my childhood. Even with

his funny habits, my dad has always done everything he could to support me in my passions.

"Do you have any clients yet? For your business idea, I mean."

I can't tell if he's asking because he wants to test my commitment, or if it's to start a lecture on needing to stick to something once I've started it. "No, but I've reached out to a bunch of people and started posting in some groups on social media. And I signed up to take a class in psychology and functional skills."

"Did you decide all this before or after quitting the drugstore?"

And he caught me. "Before. Just two days."

He shakes his head. "MacKenzie Sullivan, you've got to stick with something long enough to find out if it's something you want to do."

"Which is why I want to do this. Having my own business will be just what I need. I can work the hours I want and not have to answer to anyone."

"You think starting a business is going to be that easy?" he asks, folding his arms across his chest. "That you'll be off at five o'clock every day and won't have to spend extra time to get paid?"

I mirror his pose, giving me a feeling of control. "No, I've looked up a lot of info, done my research for this. I mean, it would be a lot easier to start with a ten-thousand-dollar cushion in the bank, but I've got to start somewhere."

"What would you use the money for if you had it?" Interrogation 101.

I focus on emptying the box to give me time to think. "I'd use it to advertise."

"Where, when, how?"

Seconds tick by and I let my arms drop to my sides. "All right. I guess I need to do more research."

"Good. Never stop learning." My dad glances up at me and says, "Why don't you come by the house this weekend? I'd be honored to be your first client."

I can't help but let my jaw drop open at his comment. "You want me to organize the house?" Was I sent to another time-line? I'm not sure I can hack it in the multiverse, so I hope I'm just hallucinating.

It's been at least six years since I've been to my childhood home. I'd decided to go through my father's storage shed out back one winter break, hoping to get rid of some of the excess and allow us to store real equipment and supplies back there. It's a crazy idea to store the cars we drive in the garage, like normal people. A large box of comics had been ruined by water and mold, so I'd tossed them out, not thinking it would matter.

That started a fight that lasted several months between me and my dad. We've smoothed things over, but I haven't set foot in the house since college started back up that year.

He presses his lips into a thin line and says, "It's been too long since you kept me in check. I don't need anyone reporting me to the city and condemning the house."

I frown. "Dad, please say it's not *that* bad."

"It's not *that* bad, but it's darn close."

That's not a good sign. My mind calls up the hallways and bedrooms, likely filled with junk. And if my dad is admitting a problem, it's probably a lot worse than he's making it sound. "What if I come tomorrow after my mud run? I don't have much this coming week, so it will be a good start."

He's quiet for a moment before he says, "The rink isn't the typical place for people needing that type of business, but you could always make some cards with your phone number on them. Maybe someone will pick one up."

I grin and walk over to the satchel bag I carry as a purse. "I just got them in the mail today. Here you go."

I hand my dad a small stack of white and black business

cards. They follow the aesthetic I want to give as an organizer, simple and to the point.

"What's with the squiggly box on the back?" he asks, turning it over.

"It's a QR code, Dad. I have it directed to a simple website I built last week. From there, people can connect to my social media platforms and see what I've done in the past."

It takes a minute for me to show him how to scan the code and go to the site.

"It's kind of blank, don't you think?" he says, using his thumb to scroll up. "I mean, I know you're working on it, but you might need some place holder pics. And your Quickstagram says you haven't posted any pictures yet."

With a laugh, I nod. "Yeah, I'll take some before pics and then some afters of your house and post them. It can show the extreme side of organizing."

"Well, bring all the cleaning supplies you have. I'm out."

Of course he is. Even though my irritation that he keeps living among trash and junk is rising, there's a slight thrill at seeing him put my business cards right next to his, the ones people take when they want to schedule a party or an event at the rink.

"Do you know how amazing you are, Dad?"

He blushes and shakes his head, avoiding eye contact. "I didn't have much to give you growing up, not like your mom did."

A pang of sadness hits me. He always beats himself up over my parents' divorce. "I didn't need everything. I just needed you cheering me on. Every time I looked up into the stands, you were there. Supporting me. Encouraging me. Junk only heightens my anxiety, but knowing I had someone to be there when I fell, that was more than all the presents in the world."

He gives a small laugh and says, "Someone had to keep you

grounded, otherwise your ego would've taken you to the clouds. At least your three brothers could help me in that area."

We both laugh at this. His words are too true to debate.

"You've turned into one tough cookie, Mac. I admire your courage in starting this."

"You have to promise you won't get mad at me for getting rid of things." I give him a side-eyed look so he knows I mean business. "And that you'll call me Kenzie."

With a resigned tone, he nods and says, "I promise."

As if in response to his answer, several of the shin guards fall off the wall, taking down anything hanging below them.

"I'm taking that as a sign," I say, laughing at Dad's surprised expression.

He uses his fingers to cross over his chest and says, "I solemnly swear I'll get rid of the junk."

I can barely breathe after laughing that much. Once all the gear is situated on the wall again, I say, "I'm going to head out."

"Here's money for the supplies," Dad says, pulling out a couple twenties. "See you later, Kenz."

"Thanks, Dad. Decide what you want to keep. We'll get everything figured out tomorrow."

I've got my first job. It might take me about twenty years until it's finished, but it's a start.

2

TREY

Who knew finding someone to spend your life with was so hard? Obviously, I'd bought into the lie that when the time was right, Ms. Perfect-For-Me would stroll up and say, "Hey, I think we're in this for the long haul."

Okay, that's not the most eloquent of phrases, but I wouldn't mind that right now. It might be the off-season for hockey, but I've still got a lot of training to do to stay in shape. Dating as a professional athlete isn't the easiest with cameras following me around either.

It's summer and I see couples everywhere. They're holding hands, kissing, and even calling each other weird pet names. I'm not into that type of thing, but I feel like I'm missing out on all the secrets of life because my track record for love keeps breaking down before it even leaves the station.

My parents were the classic fall in love at first sight and live happily together for the next forty years, raising me and my three sisters. They'd met at the State Fair when my father was working one of the booths and went on their first date that night. Fast forward a whole month to their engagement and then their marriage six weeks later.

My dad always says, "When you know something, you don't wait to act on it."

I don't think I was given that gift.

And now I'm grumpy because I'd been sucked in by one of those social media videos about the success of people who get up early to get their morning started, and last night I was all motivated. Now I'm wishing I'd turned off my alarm and slept until a normal hour. I haven't had to get up before sunrise since college.

One thing getting up early is good for is getting all the little things done, but I'm dragging. I might have to get a coffee after crossing off the next item on my to-do list: Get my skates sharpened.

Do I make lists often? No. I'm definitely not conquering the world either.

I park my car in a space away from the door of the Alvey Ice Rink. The Breeze rink has just about everything I could want, except for Brian, the guy who's basically a professional at skate sharpening. I've taken my skates to him ever since I started playing in the NHL because he always did such a great job when I came to camps at this rink. I grab my skates out of the trunk and my phone rings as I shut it.

It's Dave, my agent. He's been working on some endorsement deals for me, which would be nice to fill the time after I'm done with training every day.

"Hey Dave," I say, walking toward the door.

"Trey. Okay, I've got some amazing deals for you. The hockey company, Bauer, wants you to be in a few of their commercials coming up. It will only take a half-day to film and do voiceovers. That will happen closer to season. The second deal is for a local matchmaking company. You'll meet the owner of Love, Austen next Monday around lunchtime at their offices." Dave has never been one to waste words.

"I'm excited about the Bauer endorsement but what is Love, Austen?" I ask. I lean against the wall next to the doors to finish the conversation.

"I just told you. It's a matchmaking company. They're filming a docuseries on how the whole process works and you'll get to be one of the main people they follow."

My stomach sinks at the news and I stop, trying to register his words. Now that company name is familiar. My teammate, Carson Carver was on their reality show, *The Suitor*, a few years ago. He reconnected with his childhood sweetheart and now they're living the dream. Two adorable kids and a relationship to envy. They are the reason I've had this restless feeling about settling down. I need someone who will help me navigate life as an adult while also not making me feel like she's controlling everything. My mom is a pro at that and while I love her to pieces, I'm twenty-eight and need some room to breathe.

"You know I'm the worst at being filmed when I'm not talking about hockey. This will be like watching a plane crash."

"Well, they're willing to take a chance on you. You might even get your wish."

"What wish?" Dave and I know a decent amount about each other, but that's mostly for business purposes, not for wedding bells.

"To have a family."

Doubtful.

Everything in my brain is warring and I feel like a small child ready to throw a tantrum. Instead, I take a deep breath. "If I don't like anything about the show or their plans for it, I'm walking."

Dave laughs and says, "That's just fine, man. Seriously. The owner is pretty chill and the whole operation seems like it works. If I wasn't already married, I'd be tempted to give it a try."

Even though Dave has been my agent for several years, I'm not sure if I can take that as truth or him trying to ease my worries about the whole thing.

"Fine. I'll be there Monday. See you there."

"I have to go on vacation with the in-laws. My wife has already threatened many things if I don't go. Or take my phone. There's a lot going on here."

I shift from one leg to the other, trying to wrap my brain around the idea. "So much going on that you forgot about signing me up for a matchmaking service?"

"Marriage is a juggle, man. My wife went out of town for a few days and I have to say, she must be Superwoman or something because I don't know how she does it all."

"That might be a sign for you to step in more often," I say, laughing. It's least something to get my mind off promoting a matchmaking website. How am I supposed to do that?

I've never had trouble finding a date for the various events I have to go to, but most were there for the pictures that made it to the headlines, not for anything long-term.

Maybe talking to Carson would be a good idea. He'd have some inside information that would help me feel at ease, especially with the cameras. Or turn it all down.

My phone rings again, and to my surprise, it's my friend Spencer. I doubt the man has ever seen seven in the morning.

"Spencer, what's–"

"I forgot some tennis shoes. Will you bring an extra pair if you haven't left yet?"

My brain is reeling as I'm trying to figure out what he means. "Left for what? I'm heading to get my skates sharpened."

"The mud run, remember? We all signed up to do it on Dani's orders."

I only vaguely recall them talking about a mud run, but not that it was this morning. "I didn't sign up for anything."

Spencer groans. "Dude, we knew you'd forget. I signed you up but you have to get on the highway now to meet us there."

Shaking my head, I say, "I'm not doing a mud run. I have things to do." I glance down at the list I made. There isn't anything pressing, but I don't need Spence to know that.

In a voice that's lower and closer to the phone, Spencer says, "Jack bet that you wouldn't show. Come on, man. You owe me for setting you up on that last date of yours, the one for the charity auction. I can't lose a bet to Jack today."

As much as I want to say I'm sick and have to get back to the house to recover, he's right. I owe him for helping me not go alone to any event. If the old ladies at those things find out I'm single, I'll have fourteen phone numbers and a wedding venue within minutes. Dates equal survival at those things.

"Fine. Send me the address. But I'm not happy about it."

"Thanks, man. You're saving me from a day of torture."

I shake my head. "Running through mud sounds worse."

Spencer clears his throat. "No, man. You haven't lost a bet with Jack in a few months, which means you're delusional at the moment. He'd make me do something ridiculous, like eat the mud or something."

I cringe, feeling a grittiness in my mouth as if I'm being forced to eat mud. "I'm coming."

Blowing out a breath, I head back to the car. This is not how I saw the day going.

3

KENZIE

Whiplash, that's what my life has come to figuratively and physically.

Things seem like they're going good for a few minutes and then wham! My head hits the back of the passenger seat for the third time on this trip and I'm ready to yell at someone.

I'm beginning to wonder if we'll make it to the mud run before we hit retirement age.

"Millie, do you want me to drive?" I ask, trying to keep the edge from my voice. When we talked about the mud run a few weeks ago, my roommate offered to drive the van she uses for work as a nanny. The one problem is I've never ridden with her before and probably won't again.

Millie looks over and shakes her head. "No, you're the map girl. I won't be able to get anywhere without the map."

I turn and look back at our other two roommates, Evie and Hillary. I widen my eyes hoping I'm not the only one internally freaking out. Are they not feeling the record-level panic I am about this hour-long car ride?

"I can navigate with the map," Evie says, leaning forward. "And if you're not driving, you won't need Kenzie's help."

How she's able to say it with so much kindness makes her look like a saint.

The Sullivan family had two volume settings while I grew up, loud and louder. Those usually involved several emotions, but at this point, I feel like steam is coming out of my ears.

We hit slower traffic, which I'd expected. Even on a Saturday morning in Boston, we've hit road construction.

Roll forward, sudden brake check. Head slamming into the headrest. Repeat.

Millie looks out on the world like a new doe, her eyes wide and all the color drained from her face.

"That might be a good idea," she finally says and I'm too stunned to move.

"Y-You want me to drive?" That little sliver of hope that I won't be killed on my way to what's supposed to be a fun race is holding its breath until she moves.

Mille nods and unbuckles her seat belt. The door is open before I've even made a move.

"Go!" Hillary says, waving for me to switch seats.

"At least it wasn't just me who was worried about the trip," I say, taking my chances over the middle console rather than going out the door.

"The poor girl just needs some more time learning how to drive in the city," Evie says. "I think she comes from a really small town."

The passenger side opens and Millie gets in, her eyes already spilling tears.

"Oh, now Millie, don't cry," I say, regretting the surge of irritation from seconds ago. "I just know what it can be like to drive in this area."

I don't usually go out as far to the middle of Massachusetts as we're going, but driving in this state is all the same. Defensive driving is the daily menu.

"I just panic when there's traffic like this. I've been here for eight months now and I can't even drive like a normal human." Millie buries her face in her hands.

Hillary leans forward, touching Millie's shoulder. "Millie, you did great. I get scared driving here too sometimes and I've lived here my whole life. Well, minus the time I was a pirate guide on a remote island." That gets the rest of us laughing.

Even though we've been best friends since high school, Hillary skipped out on her wedding without telling me, the maid of honor. She ended up on some tourist island where cruise ships dock and worked in the pirate museum. She's only lived with us for a couple months and this is the most connection she's had with Millie and Evie since moving in.

I got an apology a few weeks ago about her disappearing act, which meant I had to check Hillary's pulse to see if she was still alive. Everything I've seen from her since she moved in shows signs of her changes. Maybe that remote island was the coffee to wake her up.

Millie sniffles and nods. "Where I come from, we have maybe two stop lights in the whole town. My mom always calls me in a panic every time she hears the wail of an ambulance, thinking that I've gotten hurt or in an accident or something."

I steer the car through traffic, with Evie's guidance using my phone.

"There's a new email notification from Love, Austen. I didn't know you were part of the program." I can see Evie's curious expression through the rearview mirror.

"I was at one time, but I closed my account." Why would they be trying to email me? So many memories of my short stint with the matchmaking company flood my brain. The last thing I'd heard from them was the email, "We're sad to see you go." That was nearly a year ago. We still have at least fifteen minutes to get to the farm and now curiosity is building. "What does it say?"

Evie takes a few seconds before speaking. "Dear Kenzie, we're writing to you as a former client for our company. Ever since rolling out the matchmaking app, we've made great gains in couples all over the world—"

"Scan down. Is there a point to this?"

I slow down as the car in front of me is practically crawling along the road.

"It says below that they are wanting you to take a survey to help them change some things. Every submitted survey will be given a $100 gift card."

My bank account practically screams at me to fill out the survey. There's no way I need my roommates to find out how low on cash I am. I shrug and say, "Thanks. Where do I need to go from here?"

We finally drive into the parking lot and I can see a few of the obstacles set up. Excitement mixes with adrenaline through me. Getting dirty isn't always my idea of fun, but this is one of those things I thought my roommates could do with me to cross it off the bucket list. Lists are my thing. They help my brain focus by getting all the information on the page.

"How's work going, Kenzie?" Evie asks. It's been at least a week since I've seen everyone. They work at all hours for their various jobs and I haven't had a chance to explain about my change of occupation.

"Well, I quit the drugstore and...I'm starting an organizational business."

There is a long moment of silence and then Evie and Hillary start talking at once, while Millie gapes at me from the passenger seat.

"That's awesome, Kenzie," Evie says.

"You're an expert in that area already," Hillary says.

"I don't have much of a portfolio," I say, gripping the wheel to turn into the small dirt parking lot. "I just hope to get a few people to start with and then get the referrals going."

I see Evie and Hillary stare at me through the rearview mirror.

"I'm surprised you haven't been taking pictures of every time you clean our house," Hillary says with a grin.

Nodding, I say, "I should've. But people would notice that all the pictures are practically the same."

I glance out the window. There's color everywhere. I've always been a sucker for bright colors, but this is like a dopamine rush.

"Okay, let me go check in," I say, giving the keys to Millie.

I walk over to the main table, almost skipping that we're here. Alive. Early. My brain is doing its own victory dance. And I'm free from having to talk about the matchmaking situation.

If they want a filled survey, I'll give them one. And then I'll make sure to leave a lengthy paragraph about how the men using this app are complete tools who shouldn't play with hearts.

The woman behind the table glances up and says, "Name?"

"Spice House," I say. It's the name I gave our small house and its occupants because we pretty much make up every spice there is with the different personalities. Some sugary sweet, i.e., Millie and Evie. Me as the chili pepper, usually when things are overwhelming, and Hillary is Italian seasoning flavored. Dani, before she married Miles, was the garlic seasoning. You can never have too much.

"Here's your packet. I've got listed here that eleven people are on your team. Is that correct?"

"I'm sorry, did you say eleven? We're only supposed to have seven." Me, Millie, Evie, Hillary, Dani, Miles, and Landon, the husband of our landlord and former roommate, Rachelle.

"If you give the link to more people, they are allowed to sign up under your team," the woman says smugly.

She hands me the paper that lists the names and my stomach drops.

There are the seven of us who'd planned to make it. Rachelle didn't want to risk her pregnancy at twelve weeks, which is totally understandable.

Then Drew, Spencer, and Jack, along with the one name I'll break out into hives if I ever see in real life again.

Trey Hatch.

4

KENZIE

Of all the friend groups Dani had to marry into, why couldn't they have been ugly and unwilling to do anything but play video games?

Okay, so Trey is friends with Miles, which means Dani is friends with him. But she knows about my insane knowledge of his hockey career after Miles set us up with box seats to the Breeze playoff game a few weeks ago. Maybe the guys have to jump on the bandwagon, as a sort of friend code. But I don't have to be happy about it.

I take the bag of shirts and walk over to my little carpool.

"Did you all know we have extra team members?" I put a hand on my hip and stare at each one of them.

Guilt. It's carved into their expressions.

"Dani thought it would be good to invite the guys," Evie said with a small smile.

I frown. "Why didn't she ask me first?"

I have to take a deep breath. I can't control everything, but it's not that hard for me to be reasonable when people are upfront about things. Sure, I would've said no if Dani had asked, but that's neither here nor there.

"Because she knew you'd be like this," Hillary says, waving her hand up and down in my direction.

Miles pulls up in his black car and out steps Dani, as well as Spencer and Jack.

I blow out a breath, relieved Trey isn't with them. He's the last person I want to see right now. My brain needs to focus on the race, not be constantly distracted by the guy.

Except he drives up right then. And all the cute swear words, he looks good. His dark hair seems to fall perfectly whereas my messy bun needs to be fixed.

I hand out the shirts to the team and give the rest of them to Dani to give to the guys. I'm acting like a female neanderthal, but this whole morning has thrown me off my groove.

"Thanks for putting this together, Kenzie," Spencer says. He pulls on his t-shirt and it's several sizes too small. He's got one arm sticking up in the air and the rest is bunched up around his middle.

The others laugh and I grin, shaking my head. "Spencer, don't you know you're supposed to check the size before putting it on?" I walk over and help him out of the shirt, managing to smack myself in the face once the shirt inches past his shoulder blades. My nose burns and my eyes have to blink several times to stop seeing stars.

"You all right?" Trey asks.

"Great, just amazing." I try to smile even though I'm hurrying to wipe away tears so I don't look like I'm crying. That wall hasn't been breached in months, and I won't let the dam go because this morning isn't how I thought it would be. At least my nose doesn't start bleeding.

Dani switches out Spencer's shirt. "Sorry, I gave you mine." They laugh and put them on, the new sizes working much better.

"We'll need to get started over here," I say, pointing toward the start line.

"Okay, Kenz," Jack says, coming a bit closer. I see Hillary shrink away in my peripheral vision, but tuck that away to ask about later. "What are we playing for?"

I frown. "For the enjoyment of running through mud without having to clean up at home."

"No, there's got to be something to up the ante. Something that pushes us to win. Maybe eating something gross, or singing in Harvard Square in a bathing suit."

The group laughs and I keep my gaze on Jack's, folding my arms over my chest. Of the whole guy group, Jack is the one who likes to poke and prod to get a reaction. I'm not about that just now.

"Are you talking about a bet?" I ask.

Jack nods. "For sure. Whoever wins gets to decide the consequence of the other."

I shrug. "Okay, what do you have in mind?"

"What about a date night with everyone?"

I laugh, the sound coming out hysterical. I promise I'm not a witch.

"No dates."

Jack frowns and says, "Why not? I thought for sure you'd be up for some fun."

I wave to the course and say, "If you hadn't figured it out yet, this is my idea of fun. Dates are on the blacklist of life."

Miles laughs and says, "What's with you ladies and your lists?"

He has a point. Rachelle had her breakup bucket list to help her get over Landon and while I don't think Dani had one in particular, she's been known to write down whatever comes into her brain. I glance at Evie and Hillary, wondering what kind of list people they would be. Millie I've got pegged as just hoping to make it alive one day at a time.

"Don't you worry, we have lists for everything."

Jack takes a step toward me and turns, so he's facing the

same direction but he's on my left side. "What kind of lists are we talking about?"

He put his fingers up to his chin as if thinking on some deep topic.

"Stuff, okay. Let's go get ready for the race."

I don't need him to find out how deep my obsession for writing down goals or wishes goes, or who might be featured in some of them. Like his hockey buddy who is watching the exchange as if at a tennis match.

"If we're betting, I need to know what the stakes are," Jack says, and I'm ready to throw a punch. The guy isn't usually bad, he's just grating on my nerves at the moment.

"How about the winner gets to choose the consequence. But no dates."

Trey and Spencer give each other a frown and Trey says, "Are you sure you want to keep that open-ended?"

It takes me back to the movie Pirates of the Caribbean, where Elizabeth Swan uses the pirate code to ask for Will Turner to be released. Or maybe it's herself when she's first taken? I can't remember.

What kind of trick would Jack spin off my words?

"No dates, and the consequence can't be that we have to do anything sans clothes." My cheeks redden at that thought and I make sure not to look in Trey's direction. My whole body will burn to ash if I think of him in even his underwear.

Confidence soars through me. I've got speed, and I know that even if I do come in second place, I can handle just about anything they're bound to dish out as long as I'm fully clothed.

Well, maybe not from Jack.

A bunch of cheers pulls me from the memory and I turn to find Trey walking to stand next to me. Gosh, why does the man have to look so dang hot all the time?

I've been able to keep my decade long crush for the guy a secret so far, but I'm a little nervous about how I'll be able to keep up the charade if we're constantly doing things as a big friend group. The least my roomies could've done was to give me a heads up. No, maybe it's better they didn't say anything. I would've gone through every scenario possible and panicked for days. I might've feigned sick this morning instead of coming here.

Turning away, I head to the start line. There's a big crowd and maybe I won't tip off my friends that I'm flustered by the hockey star.

Not that he would remember the chubby, scrappy hockey girl who attended a few camps with him growing up. There wasn't even a hint of knowing who I was when we met up with him after his game. If he knew I was the same girl as Mac-Attack, would he be weirded out?

One of my lists is the top twenty reasons Trey should be put in the hall of fame, and he's only been playing for four years in the NHL. He's the hometown hero alongside Carson Carver— working to build the Boston Breeze and help them win a Stanley Cup Championship.

I'm obsessed in a weird way. No, I don't stalk him at his house, just admiring from afar. That was until my new best friend Dani had started dating Miles. Oh man, it's a mess. I'm a mess.

"Hey," a voice says next to me. We're squished into a big mob of people getting ready to start the race when I turn and nearly fall to the ground.

Drew Evans is standing there with a smile on his face. He does it on purpose because of our brief history together.

Before I moved into the Spice House, I rented an apartment in a building he owns. One of the kind old ladies on a different floor felt sorry for me one day after I'd been dumped by my ex-fiancé. So, she concocted this crazy plan to force me to have breakfast with the owner of the building by pretending her plumbing needed to be fixed. He wasn't too excited about the ambush and I try to play it cool around him, but it's awkward.

I've got a lifetime of those to recount.

"Hey, Drew. I didn't know you got invited."

He nods. "I've always wanted to try this and figured it would be fun. Landon was hoping I'd be here to run with him." I turn to look at the sidelines. Tiffany has a beautiful toddler in her arms and Rachelle is holding her stomach in that typical pregnant lady pose.

My heart twinges a bit. Will I ever have that chance? I need commitment in a relationship, which isn't something the guys I attract have as a personality trait. That's why dating is off the table. I'm done. I'll just give the matchmaking company the official stamp of disapproval when I leave this course. Because I can't turn down a gift card for a fifteen-minute questionnaire.

"Well, I'm glad you could make it." I turn around, focusing on the time clock at the top of the starting arch and breathe out. I know this isn't a marathon or anything, but I might be a bit competitive. "Jack has called for a bet."

"That should be interesting. Everything I know about him is all second-hand."

"Kenzie," another voice says from the side, "What are you doing here?"

I turn, letting out a little whimper. One of my exes, Johnny Sutherland, stands two people over with a wide grin on his face. What is happening to me? Why do I have to face everyone I've dated or had awkward encounters with at this rural mud race?

Please don't let Donovan be the next one I see.

We are in the middle of nowhere Massachusetts and none of these people have ever been interested in the things I've liked. I can't really count Drew in that because there was never true interest. But Johnny here? The guy would've been fine to become part of the couch because he watched so many sporting events on TV. I love to watch a good game, but after a couple of hours, I go stir crazy.

"Obviously I'm here to run a race. And you?" I ask Johnny.

He grins. "I figured I'd tag along with my girl," he says, wrapping his arms around a very attractive woman in the shortest shorts I've ever seen. How's she going to run in those? I'd be picking wedgies throughout the entire course.

"Good for supporting someone," I say, turning slightly before I say, "for once."

I glance around, crossing my fingers I don't see another person I've dated. That's not what my life needs at this point.

To be honest, the rest of the balls I've been juggling have hit the ground at least twelve times. I'm lucky to have two still in the air: my roommates and my sanity. Well, that last part is questionable. I'll probably be wishing I hadn't agreed to clean up my dad's house when I go look at it later today.

The group shifts as the clock winds down for the last minute before our heat heads out into the mud. My group is now surrounding me and I force a smile, trying to keep the overwhelm of emotions from exploding from me. Sure, they might irritate me on some levels, but having people to support me, even in something like this is gratifying.

I didn't think I'd ever find people who would go along with anything I suggested. But since the moment I moved into the Spice House, I've been accepted for my cleaning quirks and my chocolate obsession.

And then, as if fate is laughing at me thoroughly, a handsome brown-haired guy comes to stand next to me.

"Do you think we'll win?" Trey asks with a wink. Gosh, why does this guy have to be so charming?

"I'm not sure about you, but I think I can handle it," I say, keeping my eyes forward so I don't start to smile. I cannot fall for this guy. That downward spiral would not be pretty.

"Well, it might be a team effort to beat Jack. Have you

decided what you want to assign as the punishment after the win?"

Why does the way he says that make me all fluttery? Ugh, I need some Trey Hatch immunity pill.

"Not yet. But I'm sure I'll come up with some ideas by the end of the race."

I hop back and forth a bit, hoping to hide the nerves from how close he is as just a normal warmup routine.

"You never told me why you were so bugged that day we met at the arena."

His statement catches me off guard and I turn, just as the gun goes off for our heat. The mob passes us, and half of me wants to sprint to catch up while the other wants to see what he actually remembers about that day at the rink. Or any days for that matter.

"I've just admired your skills on the ice for a long time, and was surprised that you could be so egotistical in thinking everyone has something they want signed."

Trey laughs. "That's all most people want me for anyway."

I'm surprised by the bitterness in his voice and try to come up with something to say before he starts jogging.

"How about we start over? Hi, I'm Trey and I don't like mud."

I tilt my head to the side, as if that will give me a better view of him. I'm right, it just sends my stomach doing flips at the sight of his strong jaw and attractive lips.

"We better hurry. There's no way I'm letting Jack win this thing," I say, jogging toward the first obstacle. He joins right next to me and I say, "You don't like mud and you still signed up to come?"

He shakes his head. "Spencer and Jack signed me up, at Dani's request."

I search the horizon for Dani and frown. "She's going to hear about it."

"What do you mean?" Trey asks, looking confused and a bit hurt. "You didn't want me to come? Or the whole group?"

Blowing out a breath, I've managed to screw up a lot in the three hours I've been awake, but something about his expression has me wanting to throw my arms around him and pull him in for a hug. Must resist.

"I, uh, just didn't expect all the guys to come."

We move our feet through the tires, my shoes sinking deeper in mud with every step. At least I tied my shoes on tight enough that they aren't sliding off completely.

"So, Kenzie, what do you like to do?" His breathing is barely more than a normal pace and I'm doing all I can to get air into my lungs as we run to the next section.

"Let's catch up before we can't make up the distance. Then we'll chat."

I lengthen my strides, trying to block out the strange sensation of the drying mud on my legs.

The sooner I get this over with, the higher the chances I'll leave with my dignity intact. I don't want to see his face when he finds out who I am.

5

TREY

Mud. This is a different kind of training for me, but so far, it's been kind of fun. Seeing Kenzie again has me distracted from the feel of the gritty substance that is already up my legs.

I know, hockey isn't a clean sport, but at least I can get my gear washed every few weeks. I'm afraid I'll be cleaning mud and sand out of my clothes and shoes for the next month.

Kenzie picks up the pace, pushing me to run faster. There's one part of her banter with Jack that I'm curious about.

"Why were you so adamant about no dates with Jack?" I ask.

She laughs, shaking her head. "Dates and I aren't a good combination. I'm cursed to be single forever."

"Please," I say, taking a couple breaths in between words. She's pushing even faster and I'm motivated by the challenge of keeping up with her. "It's all a matter of perspective."

"Was it bad to make a bet with Jack?" Kenzie asks, changing the subject.

"He comes up with the worst punishments. He took inspiration from the How to Eat Fried Worms book and made Owen eat them for fourteen days a couple years ago."

Kenzie frowns. "Who's Owen?"

I'm breathing kind of heavily but manage to say, "He's one of our... friends from way back. He's been... on a few medical mission... trips lately."

We jump over a large pipe and into a bog covered in barbed wire.

Kenzie and I pass several of the team but I've still got my eyes focused ahead on Jack. The man can move about as well as the animals he takes care of on a daily basis.

"Ow!" I hear from the side and see that Kenzie's ponytail is stuck in the barbed wire. Every time she moves, it only pulls more.

I look forward to my opponent and decide I can pause a few moments to help. As much as I want to beat the team, I don't want Jack to win more. And leaving her here to face whatever punishment he doles out would make the guilt that much worse if I can spare her from it.

"Hold still," I say, trying to stay below the barbed wire until I make it to her.

"I'm fine. Go so you don't lose."

"Don't worry, I don't plan to lose. But it would be better to have you by my side while we cross the finish line." I tug at the hairband that got caught on the barb and free her from the obstacle. Guilt at leaving her there would eat me alive. "Then we can both come up with something for Jack."

She crawls through the mud until she's free from the obstacle before she turns her head to say, "Thank you." The woman is ditching me after I saved her.

Maybe I've been connected to the wrong girls before, the ones who stick to my side like glue for a photo op. This feels different, almost like she's not only trying to catch up with Jack, but that she's running away from me. She's an anomaly for sure.

Which means I need to kick up the pace, for no other reason than getting an answer to her no date policy.

6

KENZIE

Why should be stamped on me somewhere. Maybe I should get a tattoo of it on my forehead.

Why does stuff like this awkwardness happen to me?

"Hey babe. Looking good with all that mud."

I don't have to turn to see Johnny getting ready to climb the mountain of wet dirt next to me.

"Not your best compliment, Johnny."

"I'm just saying, I've never seen you look this good."

I grit my teeth and try to let the backhanded compliment slide away. Instead, it's like an ax in a tree trunk.

"Goodbye, Johnny." I climb the mountain, using sheer will to propel me up the slippery slope.

While I want to celebrate the fact that I've lost a few dozen pounds since Johnny and I dated, it makes me sick that it's the first thing he notices.

I slide down the other side, right into a pool of muddy water, that's actually deeper than I originally thought. And in my panic, I swallow a large mouthful, making me shudder as I try to make it back to the surface.

I swim to the edge and look up as a hand moves into view. Trey.

"I've got it," I say, pulling myself out of the water. He's already saved me once and I don't need him to do so after every obstacle. Thank goodness I decided on the tight yoga pants today because I don't need to give anyone a show.

I don't look at him as I start running. This section is a longer run on a trail with less mud.

"Who was the guy?" Trey asks, keeping pace with me.

I push my legs harder, seeing Jack several lengths ahead of me.

"What guy?" I ask, hoping he didn't hear the conversation I had with Johnny.

Trey jutted his thumb back and says, "The one back there on the slide."

"An ex-boyfriend." The hope that I could actually stamp out that part of my history is strong. If only I'd learned my lesson long before this.

We're both silent for several minutes, the sound of feet pounding on the ground and our breathing filling the space. It's strange to be comfortable enough to not have to fill the silences.

"Is he your type?" Trey's words bounce around in my head a bit before they sink in.

I shake my head, trying to conjure a mental picture of "my type" but all I see is Trey and I have to shake my head. Not going to happen, Kenz.

"My *type* leans toward lug heads who've got eyes only for big chests, no waist, and so much makeup they could be in a theater production." I wish saying that out loud made me feel better.

"Well, that's one way to classify him," Trey says with a laugh.

"Hence why I don't date anymore." The words come out

breathy, but not because I'm struggling for air. It's a weird time trap that I'm here talking to the guy of my dreams about what my type is.

He doesn't fit into the lug head category, at least I hope not. From my quick studies of his dates throughout the years, he doesn't seem to have a type.

"You haven't had one fun date in your life? Ever?" Trey gives me a look that he doesn't believe me.

I shuffle through several of my past dating experiences and shake my head. "No, they either consist of the guy wanting to make out the entire date, or someone who leaves me with the check. I'm willing to go in halfsies just to have a good conversation and not leave a sour taste in my mouth."

Trey smiles and I have to pull my gaze away or I could get sucked into that vortex. "So you are open to dating then. Have you heard of a matchmaking company called–"

"Love, Austen?" I ask, cutting him off.

His smile falls and he slows down. "Yeah, how did you know about them?"

"We don't know each other enough for that conversation, Hatch."

"I'm supposed to be on a docuseries about matchmaking. You should join me." We're walking at this point, and I decide to push to a jog. Movement helps me when I can't come to a quick decision on things.

I raise my eyebrows. "Why? Because we're suddenly such good *friends?*"

That's probably not the best tone to use, but I don't want to even ponder friendship with this man. We were kind of friends as teens, but some guys can't get over the fact that a girl can play the same sport they do. And I'm safe in the unattached zone when it comes to the Trey Hatch orbit.

"You have a calming effect on me, which is strange because you seem to be agitated every time I'm around, like after my game. But I think that would help me out to get through the camera time."

"Calming effect? Me? Yeah, I don't believe that. I'm not putting myself through misery again." I pause, his words finally registering. "What do you mean help you get through camera time?"

He gives me a sheepish grin and says, "If it's not related to hockey, I don't do well with a camera in my face. All the videos my mom took of me growing up are of me covering the lens with my hand or running away."

Surprising information.

"I can pay you for your time," he says.

Shaking my head, I say, "Don't you have guy friends for that?"

He frowns. "I do have guy friends, but relationship stuff is kind of touchy these days. Ever since Miles got married, the rest of the pack is feeling the pressure."

"There's no timeline to be married by. I already checked."

He bursts out laughing, as if I've just said the funniest thing ever. "Like there's some rule book on whether you'll die an old maid or old bachelor?" When I don't answer, he says, "Think about it. Please."

"Fine. Now can we keep going?" I ask, waving to the course ahead of us.

"If we push it, we can make it to the next obstacle almost at the same time as Jack."

I glance up and see that we've fallen behind again. Speed isn't something I lack, but he might be overestimating our progress a bit.

"Looks like Drew is right behind him." Dani is a few steps after the two of them, and then there's Miles. The guy is a freaking saint even during a race. Too bad he doesn't come with a brother. A duplicate of that man might get me to forget my feelings for the guy running along beside me.

I push even further, my lungs burning with the effort and the leftover muddy water residue. The next obstacle is a padded platform that moves back and forth. It resembles the set up I remember from the show *Wipe Out*.

I jump on it and then have to wait several seconds for my balance to adjust to the jarring movements. Then I rush forward, jumping to the next platform. It's a large wall and every so often, a large boxing glove juts out.

Timing it to where I by-pass all of them with ease, I think I'm in the clear until I hear "Ow," and then a splash.

I turn back to find Trey floating on the top of the water. Do I leave him to himself there?

I sigh, knowing that my awkward teenage crush won't let me do that and that he's already helped me out of a few sticky spots in this race.

Heading back to the muddy water, I jump in to drag Trey back to land. Even though I can't see his beautiful blue eyes, his face is relaxed. What if this became a reverse Snow White story and kissing him would wake him up? I shake my head. I've been reading too much fantasy lately and it's seeping into my thoughts.

Blood comes from a gash at the side of his eyebrow. I swipe at the muddy water trying to mix with the red. We'll have to get this washed out before infection sets in.

How did he sustain a cut when it was a padded glove? I glance up to see that the glove has a hole in its padding and the metal bar hit him straight on.

Crap, what are the signs of a concussion again? I'm momentarily distracted by his handsome face and have to snap out of it. I should be helping him, not relishing in this fantasy.

There's nothing around that I can press into the cut to stop the bleeding. Do I let it bleed and try to get him to the finish line and the medical tent? It takes several tries before I can rip off a section of my t-shirt but at least I get a long strip. Or what I thought was a long strip. When I try to put it around his noggin, it only reaches halfway.

I press the cloth into his wound and then stretch it down toward his neck, tying it tight there. Okay, hopefully that stops the bleeding.

Looking around, there are still dozens of people running through the obstacle, most of them not even noticing we're lying here.

Uh, this is not how I thought this morning would end.

Trey is several inches taller than me and has more bulk than even this weight-lifting gal can manage for a half-mile. But I can't just leave him here.

"Hey!" I call out, trying to get someone's attention. "Hey! Can you get the medical team?"

It's like I'm yelling at a glass wall because no one turns toward me.

A moan comes from Trey and his eyes flutter open. Panic sets in. Here I am on the ground, cradling his head in my lap. I barely know the guy except for what I've read in the tabloids and internet articles. And his stats sheet, and... yeah, a couple hockey camps together ten years ago.

He's the untouchable for me. Johnny is the prime example of my obvious missteps over the past year as he scampers by with his hand joined together with Miss Short Shorts. There was no PDA in our short relationship. What makes the difference there?

I refocus on Trey. His eyelids flutter again and he finally opens them.

"What happened?" Trey says in a low groan.

I look down at those baby blue eyes, standing out even more with the rich brown of his hair. "You hit your head." The words came out all rushed and garbled.

He sits and presses a hand to his head. The white t-shirt has a large red spot on it now.

"What happened to your shirt?" Trey asks, blinking several times as if just waking up from a nap. I guess that's technically what it was, his momentary bout with unconsciousness.

I glance down at what is now a crop top of the race t-shirt.

"Just trying to keep up with the trends, Trey. It's not the cleanest thing, so we need to get you to the medical team and wash out your cut. The last thing I need is you getting a big infection. Are you okay to stand?"

He nods. On instinct, I hold out my hand and he takes it. I have to widen my stance to keep from falling on top of him but we manage to get to a standing position. Once he lets go of my hand, the tingles and awareness that he just touched me make my brain go into overdrive.

I pretend to be dusting off my hands and glance around. "Finish line is that way."

Trey nods and starts walking alongside me.

"How are you feeling?"

"Like I just got slammed against the boards."

"Do you think it's a concussion?" I ask, wondering if I need to do something to help him.

His walk is fine, not wobbly like I thought it would be.

"No," he says, shaking his head. There's no grimace after, so I have to assume he's right. "I've had a few of those before and I think I'll be all right."

Then the awkwardness descends. Do I run as fast as I can toward the finish line because that will help me get away from him faster? Or do I stay here and let my heart beat a bit more for every time I'm around him after this?

"Thanks for staying with me. You didn't have to."

I let out a small laugh. "All I'd see for the rest of my life was your lifeless body in the water and the headlines reading, 'Hockey star drowns on mud race course.' So yeah, it was kind of a no-brainer."

Trey flinches at first and then laughs. "You're funny. And there's something familiar about you."

I freeze, trying to force my lungs to expand and contract despite my panic. Him knowing I was the girl who followed him like a puppy dog around hockey camp would be humiliating.

"I've got one of those faces, you know?" I say, turning to see how much longer until the finish line. I can see Evie and Millie walking across it right now.

I resign myself to being at the back of our team. Catching a glimpse of Trey, I work to hide a smile. The guy is fun and more laid back than I thought he was. I might as well resign myself to having him around more often. Maybe this will be like exposure therapy. More time spent around him will help me get rid of the butterflies every time I see his handsome face.

"What do you think our punishment will be?" I ask, hoping Trey will have some more information. Time to mentally work through the consequence before I actually have to participate, would be ideal.

"No idea. I'm just hoping we won't be his servant for a week or anything."

I turn to stare at Trey. "Is he a clean freak or a slob?"

"Slob, all the way."

I shudder. "I will pay him whatever is left in my bank account to not have to do that." Thinking of my bank account has my sadness drooping even further. Nothing like humility by lack of money. And then there's Trey's proposition to help him on camera. I'm not even good at cameras. Why am I even entertaining the idea?

"I'd be willing to do that too." Trey says. He turns toward me and it looks like the bleeding finally stopped.

I raise an eyebrow. "You'd give up the many, many dollars in your bank account to avoid being Jack's butler? I only have double digits in mine, so it's not that big of a draw."

"I love Jack as a friend, but the guy is brutal."

We make it past the finish line and to the group of loud cheers.

"You guys made it," Miles says, smiling.

Dani looks almost clean from the mud, except for a few splotches on her face. The others are soaking wet, so at least there's a spot to rinse off.

"We are alive," I say, gesturing to Trey.

"What happened?" Evie and Rachelle say together.

Trey gives them a small smile and then says, "I got in a fight with one of the contestants. It wasn't a pretty sight, but Kenzie came to my rescue, thank goodness."

The group is all staring, their heads bobbing back and forth between the two of us.

When Hillary and Dani both look at me with coy expressions, I know exactly where they're going with this scenario. Hillary knows my long-held crush on Trey, and Dani probably suspects it at this point.

"Nope, not a chance." I take a few steps forward and say, "Where is the wash station? I've got dirt in places I don't want to think about."

"It's over there," Jack says, grinning. "Go wash up and we'll reveal your punishment."

"You sound like a villain who wrings his hands together at the misery of others," I say. "Is the punishment for the entire group?"

Jack shakes his head. "No, just the last two across the finish line."

7

TREY

Kenzie does not look happy about being my chaperone home. Turns out getting nailed in the head might be a concussion. I would've been fine if I hadn't collapsed by the hoses to clean us off.

"Thanks for taking me home," I say, trying to get the conversation started on the hour-drive back to the city.

"I don't see why they couldn't have one of the guys drive you home," Kenzie says, pressing on the gas to get around one of the slower cars in our lane.

"Well, I don't drive with just anyone. Jack and Spencer are constantly moving the wheel, which makes me carsick. Miles is still all lovey-dovey with Dani, and I don't need that kind of backseat entertainment. Owen is about the only one I trust, but since he's not here, you're the best option."

Kenzie shakes her head. "I think *best* option is overstating things. Driving in Boston is no picnic, but I also don't want to be on the road forever. Are you getting carsick?" she asks, leaning over for a few seconds. When she looks back at the road, she has to slam on the brakes to avoid hitting a car.

Waving my hands in the air, I say, "I'll be fine, as long as you pay attention to the road." I want to close my eyes, but I'm worried I won't be able to warn her if she gets distracted. I'm supposed to wait a while after the hit before I sleep just to make sure there's no brain injury.

The whole group had been staring at me and Kenzie when we left the medical tent with the refuel-and-keep-watch diagnosis. Another strike against waking up early. I'd burned through my breakfast calories on the race course and the low blood sugar knocked me out. The medic was trying to keep from laughing at the fact a pro athlete got hit in the head on a mud race course. I'll probably have to alert Dave about it in case anyone contacts him for more information. The media spreads rumors like a piñata at a kid's birthday party.

"Kenzie has to drive you home," Jack had said. There had been some discussion and some arguing from Kenzie, but when faced with the idea of eating fourteen ice cream cones in one sitting, an hour back to the city was the better choice.

I retrace the recent conversation back and say, "I think this is the easiest punishment Jack has ever given out after winning a bet."

She frowns. "Are you sure he's not going to come back later and say 'psych!' and give us something else to do?"

I shake my head. "No, consequences have to be doled out within a couple hours of knowing who won."

Kenzie turns to look at me. "Sounds like there's a story there."

"Nothing major. Spencer took almost two days to decide on a punishment for Miles. Because of that, Miles had to be in a meeting and couldn't participate in some flash mob Spencer had organized."

"Flash mob? Like randomly dancing as if they were in a musical?" Kenzie's amazement makes me laugh.

"I'm pretty sure that's what it looked like. I had an away game."

"So, our only punishment was to drive home together," Kenzie says. "That's not fishy at all."

I adjust so I can look at her without turning my head. My neck is a little sore already, probably from the impact of getting hit.

Kenzie makes defensive driving look like a casual day of out. The sun out the window is shining on her profile and my view could be a magazine cover. Her lips are soft and relaxed, a change from the tight frown I've seen so many times from her. The long brown hair hangs down near her shoulders. She'd practically taken a shower, with clothes on, pulling out shampoo and conditioner to wash after the race.

There's a long moment of silence between us when she asks, "So, you're working with the matchmaking company, huh?"

I purse my lips, wanting to talk about anything else. "My agent set it up."

"Why do it if you're so reluctant?" she asks, glancing over at me for a split second.

"That's a great question," I say, trying to come up with a good answer. "It would be nice to find someone and settle down. Not just someone interested in the fame of being my girlfriend and then wife."

Kenzie looks like she's seen a ghost as the color drains from her face. "Do you think it will work?"

I shrug. "I don't know. My teammate used Love, Austen and his life is close to storybook perfect."

She nods and focuses on the road. "What's on your list of qualifications for this future girlfriend of yours?" Her voice shakes a bit on those last few words, and I have to lean over to make sure she doesn't faint and then send us careening into oncoming traffic.

"Are you all right? Did you swallow too much mud?"

That gets a laugh out of her. "There might've been some accidental mud swallowing. But I'm totally fine."

We settle back in. "I don't really have a list of qualifications. I always thought it would all click once I met someone. That's how my parents describe it. They met and my dad was practically scrambling to get my mom's phone number."

I turn to study her again. "What's on your list?"

She gives me a look like I've gone crazy. "Who says I have a list?"

With a laugh, I say, "Didn't you tell the guys earlier that women make all sorts of lists?"

"I haven't thought that far ahead," she says, turning down off the main road. Houses line each side of the road. "Oh, wait, I need to take you home. Punch in your address on the phone." She hands me her phone with the maps app out and I try to remember my new address. I've only owned it for a few weeks.

She turns the car around, heading back for the main road. The way she's so focused on it makes me think she's trying to avoid the conversation. The woman is adamant about not dating people, so maybe a change of subject would make her more comfortable.

"What do you do for work?" I ask, hoping that's a safe topic.

"I'm a serial job hopper," she says, a hint of a smile playing at her lips. "I'm working to start an organizing business."

"There is so much to unpack in that sentence," I say, closing my eyes for a few seconds.

She must've seen me resting my eyes because she pushes my shoulder back and forth a few times. "Stay awake a bit longer," she says.

"Explain your employment status," I say, leaning forward to stay awake. Even with the air on full-blast, my eyelids are staging a rebellion.

"I haven't found something I loved yet. So, I figured I'd go into business for myself."

"What business?"

Kenzie pauses a moment and I wonder if she's going to say anything. "It's called The Tricky Organizer."

My mind is a bit cloudy, but I nod. "So you organize stuff. Why is it tricky?"

She shakes her head and mumbles, "Maybe I should've gone with the other name."

We stop in my driveway and Kenzie looks up at the house. "This is where you live?"

I unbuckle my seatbelt. "Yep. It's not a mansion but I loved it the first time I walked through. It's got plenty of space for a bachelor."

I push the button to the garage and Kenzie parks the car.

"I didn't expect your house to look like this," she says, staring at the mounds of boxes next to the car.

"What did you expect it to be?" I ask, getting out. I'm ready to take a nap already. Has it been long enough yet?

"Either you crash with a bunch of ex-frat guys or in some house with an indoor ice rink." She smiles at that, and I laugh, causing my head to hurt a bit.

I walk up to the door to the house and am curious why she's following me. "I'll be okay."

She raises both hands. "The instructions were to make sure you got home safely. Take some ibuprofen and relax for today." Taking a couple steps down, she turns and walks out of the garage.

"Do you have a ride home?" I ask, feeling bad. We'd been having a good conversation and I go and ruin it by pushing her away. It's a reflexive habit now, after so many years of my mom coddling me.

Kenzie points to the road. "I'll pull up a map of the bus schedule."

"Take the car," I say, nodding toward my vehicle. "We'll arrange to get it later."

Something about my words makes her pause. "I'm good. I'm supposed to go to an appointment for my new business."

"Kenzie, just take the car. I doubt you'll crash it." Despite the one brake-slamming incident, I feel relatively safe with her driving my car.

She gives me a blank expression and then walks back over. "Okay, but I'll bring it back tonight."

"Whatever works for you," I say. "Thanks again for getting me home safely. Driving with the guys would've been the worst."

With a nod, she says, "No problem. Rest up. You still have to train so the Breeze don't choke like last season." The mischievous grin on her face makes me smile. Someone who knows about hockey.

"I'll take that into consideration. Bye," I say, waving as she closes the door and pulls out of the garage. I stand there for a few more moments, going back over the strangeness of the day. The most exciting part was peeling back a layer that makes up Kenzie.

It's always nice to have a friend in my corner.

8

KENZIE

My heart still beats a mile a minute and it's been an hour since I last saw Trey. I sound like I'm part of an AA meeting although instead of alcohol, I'm trying to wean myself off the fangirl in me about one of the Breeze's best players. It's not going well.

How often do I see a professional hockey player out in the wild? Or have to drive him home?

We'd had a lot of fun during our teen years, but he doesn't even remember me. To be honest, I wouldn't recognize me either. I'd been able to get rid of the glasses and the braces by the time I made it to college, but Trey was already in the system to the NHL at that point.

I head over to the Spice House and drop off Trey's car, not wanting any questions from my dad about how I ended up with a newish car a day after talking to him about saving money. There would be a lecture for sure, although I know he's just trying to protect me.

My old rust bucket gets me to the supermarket, where I pick up cleaning supplies and then drive over to my dad's house. The gas gauge is on E, but I'll somehow make it back home. And I didn't want to tell Trey I can't pay him for using his gas.

There are brown spots in the grass when I pull up, where Dad must've had some of his junk piled for the past several weeks. At least he's tried to clean up some of the outside.

As I peek around the side of the house, I frown. There are three junk cars sitting there, probably for spare parts. I keep telling him he can just go to the junkyard to find the specific part he needs when he needs it, but he'd rather have the death traps sitting next to the house.

I go through the side door and gag upon entry. What is that smell? It's like something died in here. Even my eyes are starting to water.

My dad hasn't mentioned any new pets, so hopefully I don't have to battle more than the–

"Ah!" I scream out as my foot nudges a piece of cardboard on the floor and a pack of cockroaches emerge from it. Crap. Why does it have to be those things? They make my skin crawl long after I see them.

The kitchen is covered in boxes and garbage bags, plates with old food on them and mold. Lots of mold.

I walk into what was once the front room. Instead of seeing the couch and recliners, there are piles of newspapers, magazines, empty take-out containers, and then so much garbage. Why doesn't he throw all this stuff out weekly when the garbage trucks come by?

"Brian Sullivan!" I call out, adding irritation to my tone.

"Are you here already, Baby Girl?" my dad says, walking out of his room down the hall from the living room. The man is not that tall and he has to lift his leg nearly to his armpit to make any forward progress.

"What happened here?" I wave my arms around, searching for anything that looks familiar, but all I see is junk.

Instead of joking around like I thought he would, he

glances around at the mess and shrugs, looking like a kicked puppy. "I don't know. It was just a lot."

I bite my tongue, trying to remember the things I've learned in my online psychology class. There's an underlying reason for why people do what they do, and this is no exception. I rein in my tone and say, "Where do you want me to start?" I'm mentally hoping we can avoid the kitchen for a few hours. I'm not ready to battle the cockroaches. Yet.

He looks around again and says, "I'm not even sure. I'm sorry, Mac. If you don't have time, you don't have to worry about this."

My heart breaks for him. The man is so confident in his job at the rink, but standing before me now he looks like a shell of that man. I walk over to throw my arms around his neck. "I have time to help out, Dad, as long as you'll let me. No one should have to live like this. Let's check out the bedrooms and bathroom."

I've never been so relieved to see that the bathroom, while filled with stuff, doesn't have poop piled up in random places. I might've seen too many episodes of the Hoarders reality show back in the day. To be honest, it was the main reason why I worked so hard to keep things cleaned up after Mom left. I never wanted things to get to, well, this point.

The bedrooms have clothes piled high along with bags and bags of toys, most of them broken. It would be a five-year-old's haven, more trucks and cars than they could play with in a lifetime.

"How does the basement look?" I ask, trying to keep my tone even and the accusations out of it.

"About like this."

"Okay, are you wanting to help with this? Or do you want me to do what I used to do and just chuck stuff?"

Dad starts biting his thumbnail, which is a tell-tale sign to give him a minute to think. The urge to call up a dumpster and just get started is strong, but I wait, watching what he's going to say. I've lost him once to this debate and I don't want to go through that again.

"Will you ask me before you throw anything away?"

Asking about every piece of paper and knick-knack would mean this project will stretch on for the next three years.

"What if I give you fifteen minutes in each room to find anything you want to keep? Then I'll put the rest of the stuff that isn't garbage into piles and we'll go through them together?" The piles are something I'd started doing once I moved away to college, and even now at the Spice House. Something about seeing everything I own makes it easier to decide what to keep and where it should go.

He nods. "I can do that."

He walks into the bedroom. I want to cry at the state of the place. The man had a rough childhood with his mom leaving and his dad sinking into a deep depression. My mother left after six years together because of the mess, but even then, it wasn't to this degree. The man has scars I haven't focused on for so long that I nearly forgot about them.

"I know, I know what you're thinking." His words make me check my expression, hoping to put on a mask that won't show him how grossed out I am.

Shaking my head, I say, "Dad, it will be okay. We'll figure out what we need here and then get this all cleaned up." If only it's as easy as saying the words. This project is going to require a lot more time than I originally planned. "There's nothing here we can't fix. We've just got to take things one step at a time."

Even as I say the words, I want to dig in and get going on this. My dad deserves a home, one he's comfortable bringing people to.

"Has Sherry been here in a while?" I ask. I haven't seen my dad's long-time girlfriend in a while and he hasn't mentioned her.

With a shake of his head, he says, "No, she left a while back. Said she couldn't live like this."

Another person who'd left him. That had to be the escalation trigger. "We'll fix it this time, Dad. We'll clean up the house and then we'll have you talk to someone about everything that goes into living like this," I say, using my hands to gesture to the hoard. "There are people who can help you work through the issues."

"I'm not talking to anyone about my problems. They're mine to worry about."

And now I understand where I get stubborn about feelings. The man is a vault and I've patterned myself after him. The best defense mechanism I could come up with over the past several years.

"Let's take this one step at a time," I say.

After a quick inspection of the rest of the house, we start in the bathroom. Toilet roll tubes and moldy, wet towels are all over the place, but it could be worse. That's what I have to say as I think about the house.

It could be poop all over the walls.

It could be rotting meat left in the fridge.

It could be mold causing the house to deteriorate.

My gag reflex is on point and I have to head out and grab a mask from my car. I'm lucky I grabbed a pack from the store.

My dad picks out his toothbrush and a rubber duck from the bathroom pile.

"Um, Dad, I didn't think you still played with that," I say as a joke.

He grins and says, "It's from when you were small. You and your brothers used to fight over it every time, saying the next one in the tub couldn't use it."

The words sober me and I nod. "There wasn't much we didn't fight about."

"True, but the noise meant there were people here, and that's all I cared about."

I work for the next three hours pulling out all kinds of wet and dry materials, allowing my dad to see that I've only put garbage and items beyond use in the black garbage bags.

Once I'm able to walk in with ease, I move onto the bedroom, hoping to get the main areas at least rid of the clutter. The deep clean part will come later.

The mound next to my dad's bed is made of ratty blankets and picture frames.

"Dad, do you want to keep any of this?" I ask, making sure to make the piles so he can see exactly what's there.

He nods and starts folding up the blankets.

I press my palm to his forearm to get him to look at me. "Dad, we have plenty of blankets and more than enough picture frames in the house. These are all broken. What if we get rid of these and get you some new ones?"

I try to be soothing with my words, but his eyes glaze over, looking as though I've severely wounded him.

"I'm broken, Mac. That's why everyone keeps leaving me." A tear slides down his cheek and my stomach clenches at seeing the vulnerability.

"I'm not leaving you. I'm right here. Maybe we should pause on this for today. Why don't we go get some food?" The terror in his eyes reminds me of throwing away the comics and I know we need to take this slower.

He stares at me for several seconds and nods. "I can do that."

Blowing out a breath, I try to smile as wide as I can. There is so much to unpack from what happened today and I have to let go of the idea that I'm not going to get anything done. But the issues that caused the mess in the first place need to be eased into and dissected. It would be painful if we cleaned everything up to only have it happen again.

"How was your day today?" I ask as we get into my car. I use my middle finger to flick the glass near the gas gauge, hoping it will magically go up about two notches.

"It was really good. We sold a bunch of the equipment we unpacked, which is always a bonus." It's amazing how much the rink and hockey helps my father's mental state. We aren't near his work, but he looks ten years younger and ready to head into the arena as if nothing is wrong with his living situation. "How was the mud run?"

That's a loaded question.

"It was an adventure. Dani ended up inviting her husband's group of friends. Trey Hatch got a concussion and I had to drive him home." Crap, I shouldn't have mentioned Trey.

"You were Trey's driver, huh? What did you think about that?"

I shake my head, not wanting him to tease me about this. "I was just trying to keep the guy coherent, Dad. And I have no flirting skills, so there isn't anything juicy to report."

The car jerks and then stops in the middle of the road.

"What's wrong?" Dad asks, leaning over to check the dashboard.

"Great question." I slide down into my seat as I say, "We just ran out of gas."

Dad rolls his eyes and says, "Kenzie, you're supposed to tell me when you're in dire straits. I may not have a handle on my living situation, but I have enough money to help you out when you're in need."

"Dad, I'm in dire straits." I try to keep my face neutral but a smile creeps in and we both laugh.

"Okay, let's get your car pulled over to the side of the road and then we'll figure out what to do about gas."

There's a gas station about a mile away and we talk on the way there and back, mostly about what's been happening in the hockey world. He's always seeing faces from the past at the rink.

Once we're back at my car, Dad reaches out and hands me a few twenty-dollar bills. "Here's this. Make sure you talk to me next time."

"I don't want to be a burden. I'm old enough to have my life figured out, I'm just not there yet." This is not how today was supposed to go. I should be cleaning up my dad's house, not taking his money.

"I know you think that just because you're out of college and living on your own that you're supposed to have it all figured out. But that's not always the case. Sometimes it takes us longer than others to figure out what direction our lives should take. You need a better plan to try out for your business."

Seconds ticked by and I said, "I figure I need to get the minor stuff down first and then go on with it. Website, actual jobs that I've done to help others, etc. I'll still have to find another job to support me while I'm working on it, but I feel like I've gone through all the options, Dad."

"A job can be a job for a while. You don't have to quit because of something you didn't like about it. And if it's helping you get to your goals, you're tough enough to stick it out a bit longer, right? Remember Coach Weeks? You struggled to get through that first season of college because of her. But you pushed through and were even better that next season. Treat your jobs like that, if the organizing thing is really what you want to do."

Emotions pull at me and I smile, trying to tamp down the wall of tears threatening to spill out. "Thanks. I'll find something, Dad." I pause for a moment as he gets back into the car. "We can both give ourselves some grace, don't you think?"

He's quiet for a minute and then nods. "Yeah, I think we both need to understand our fears and go from there."

"And what are your fears?"

There's another long pause before he says, "Being completely alone."

My heart breaks a little at his words. "That's a tough one. Do you think that's why you buy so much stuff?"

Dad nods. "Yeah, kind of like it's filling a hole."

I reach over and pat his hand. "Well, that's a start. It's something we can work with and fix."

"And your fears are something you can fix too. It's just a matter of uncovering what you don't want anyone to see and working on it."

"We'll have to do it together then. Chances are high I won't unless I have you pushing me about it." I grin at him and feel a bit easier after talking to Dad.

We get some food and then drop him off, heading back to my house. His words echo in my brain. It might not have been a TED talk to anyone else, but his words definitely light a fire underneath me. Maybe there is still hope for my future yet.

9

KENZIE

Who knew that clothes could weigh so much? I'm back at my dad's house Monday morning, doing everything I can to get through the heap in the bedroom. Dad promised me before heading into work that he had picked out everything he wanted to keep from the bedroom.

It took some finagling, but I dropped off Trey's car the night before, and have endured a lot of teasing from my roommates since. I picture Trey's home, and aside from the not-quite-unpacked look of the garage and its many boxes, I wonder what his style is. Modern, sporty, eclectic. Probably not the trash collecting kind, at least, I hope.

The smell of body odor is only worse the more I dig into this stuff, and I have to keep the mask in place to avoid gagging.

My phone rings from an unknown number and I let it go to voicemail. I've got things to do and if people really need me, they'll either text or leave a message.

I haul out another two black garbage sacks to the side of the house. A dumpster is supposed to show up today and I'll need to use one of my half-brothers' trucks to get the clothes taken to a donation store. I'm not sure how many major hoarding jobs I'll get in the future, but these details are good to know for future possibilities.

Leaning against the banister that surrounds the back steps, I check the voicemail.

"Hi Kenzie, this is Meg with Love, Austen. I appreciate you filling out the survey about past clients. It was so helpful in what we're trying to fix here. I also have the gift card promised to you. I'll be at our office until about two and then I have to run to my daughter's checkup. I'd love to chat with you more once you come in."

The message ends. Why would she want to chat with me more?

I'd finished the survey on Friday but didn't press the send button until Sunday afternoon. They must be desperate or really on top of things to have the gift card so quickly. But I'll use it to get me through at least two weeks' worth of groceries.

The work is long and slow. I've hauled out so many bags of garbage and clothing that I won't need to work out my biceps for at least a month.

I need a break and some sustenance to help me tackle the rest of the day. There are several fast-food places a couple minutes away from my dad's house, so I grab a sandwich and sit in my car outside his house.

The dumpster is there, which will make it so I'm not moving the bags twice.

I open a new message and text my brother, Damian.

Me: Hey, can I borrow your truck tomorrow?

Knowing him, he's probably zoned out at work for another few hours. Everything should be on track for now though. This project is going to take me at least a month, unless I can get some people in to help me. My brothers would be a good option. Maybe my roommates would be willing to help for a day as well.

Damian: Sure. What for?

Me: Dad's house. He's hired me to clean it.

Damian: Really? He let you back in there?

I laugh and shake my head. One thing I love about having older brothers is that there is either fighting or laughter.

Damian: Oh, sorry. I forgot the truck has to go in to the shop for a few repairs. I'll let you know when it's out and we'll come help with the cleanup.

I'm drawn to the message from the owner of Love, Austen. A year ago, I raved about how amazing their program was. How else would I have met Donovan?

He'd been a charming sales rep and we meshed on so many things. Our love of comedy and mysteries, getting outside and enjoying nature. The one thing that is now a glaring difference was that he disliked all organized sports. Me, thinking it wasn't a big deal, conformed to that, and I'd gotten away from the weeknight hockey games with my family. The day he proposed, I thought my life was near perfect. And then he went on a work trip and came home with stars in his eyes for someone whom I couldn't compete with.

But now, as I think about him, I realize that there were some red flags I'd chosen to overlook. The guy was gone two to three weeks out of every month. That would've been like seeing distant relatives rather than my spouse. I had distanced myself from my dad and brothers, as well as my group of friends. This all imploded a few weeks before Hillary's would-be wedding, and the aftermath wasn't pretty.

I'd gone through the cycle of crying, anger, resolving to be happy and then back again.

Did we match on a lot of similar interests? Yes. But was there ever that spark of chemistry I'd expected to feel?

I search through memories, trying to find something that

validates the thought. But there's nothing. Our kisses were fun and passionate, but maybe it was lame to dream about someone knocking me into the next realm with chemistry.

Given the opportunity, would I help people avoid the situation I went through? Without a doubt.

I'll take a short detour to get that gift card and make sure Meg knows what I've been through so other women wouldn't have to endure the embarrassment and humiliation of thinking they found the one person to stand beside them for the rest of their life only to be let down.

I know that happens even without a matchmaking service, but there's got to be a way to vet people better. What if Donovan hadn't been honest with his answers on the intake form for Love, Austen? That would make a big difference when it comes to the people that match with him.

Hopefully I can help them find a solution.

10

TREY

Two days after the race, I'm starting to feel like myself again. I'd slept through most of the day Sunday and Monday, only getting up to order food—delivered to my house.

It takes me nearly an hour to figure out what to wear to a meeting with a matchmaking company. Usually, I wear a suit to any interview, but that seems a bit eager to go along with whatever the owner might have in mind for this deal.

I pick khaki pants and an emerald green polo shirt, making sure to comb my hair. It would've been nice to wear a hat instead, but that would take away from the semi-professional vibe I'm going for. Because I don't want to look too nonchalant.

Once I arrive at the Love, Austen office, I open the door to see a young woman behind the reception desk. She looks like she might be barely eighteen. Hopefully she's not the owner.

"Hi, my name is Trey Hatch. I'm supposed to be meeting with the owner?" Why can't I remember the woman's name right now?

"Yes, I've got you down. Meg will be out shortly. Just have a seat there. Do you need anything to drink?"

"I should be good. Thanks."

The woman slings a small purse strap over one shoulder and says, "Okay, then. Just wait until Meg comes out. I have to run an errand."

I take a seat where she points and glance around the room. What a peculiar setup. It's like I stepped out of modern-day Boston and have gone back several centuries.

It's several minutes later when I hear my name from the doorway. I turn and grin when I see a woman holding a baby. The little girl is drooling all over her fist.

"It's nice to meet you," I say, walking forward and sticking my hand out. The woman shakes it loosely.

"Please have a seat in here."

I step into an office with some natural light filtering through the window. Along the wall are hundreds of pictures and what looks like wedding invitations.

"Wow, that's a pretty incredible scene. It looks like an artistic move at decor."

Meg puts the baby down in a bouncer before glancing back. "Sometimes we need reminders of why we push so hard for something to happen. There are a lot of hard days in this business—people who were matched and it didn't work out as well as they would've liked. But these," she says, gesturing to the invitations, "these are what keep me going. Knowing that I've been able to help so many people find the love of their life."

Bells ring from the front of the office and Meg holds up a hand to ask for a minute as she walks around the desk. "Sorry, Laura had to run out so I'm the one on double-duty for a few minutes."

She walks into the lobby, and I pull out my phone, trying to catch up on everything I let slide this weekend.

"Welcome to Love, Austen. How can I help you?"

"Hi," a familiar voice says. "I came to pick up that gift card you left a message about. My name is Kenzie Sullivan."

My ears perk up at her name, surprised to hear that she's here at all. The woman who is against all dating whatsoever is here at a matchmaking firm.

"Yes, I have it back here in the office. Come with me."

The door opens wider and Meg flashes me a smile before rounding the desk and sorting through the heap of papers on her desk.

"You," Kenzie says, surprise in her voice.

"Me," I say, smiling wide. "What brings you here, Mud Girl?"

The corners of her lips twitch and she finally smiles. There's something between us, like a connection I can't describe. It's broken as soon as Meg speaks.

"Here is the gift card I promised. I actually wonder if you have a few minutes, Miss Sullivan? Then I can go through everything at one time."

Kenzie frowns. I glance between the two women, wondering what Meg could want to talk to her about.

With a quick movement, Kenzie sits down in the chair next to mine. "It's Kenzie."

Meg smiles. "Okay, Kenzie, Trey, I'm sure you're wondering what I've asked you here for. The Love, Austen company came out with an app over a year ago. We've had some mixed sentiment about it. The first several months was a lot of trial and error to make sure we had all the technical elements fixed. Then it was getting the right matching system in line.

"Lately, we've had several reports that things need to be changed on the app. More security through background checks and vetting the clients signing up. That gets difficult when we've reached the entire world with the app. Jorge, my amazing tech guy, is working on several fixes at the moment. But we've been approached about some publicity through the local tv show, *Everything Your Heart Desires.*"

"I'm just here for the gift card," Kenzie says, holding it up in her hand. Her face has lost all its color.

Meg laughs and nods. "Yes, you definitely deserve that. Some of the things you shared in the paragraph section of the survey," she turns to me and says, "We sent a survey out to a selection of past clients to get a better feel for why they stopped using our services."

Kenzie squirms in her seat and looks down at her hands in her lap. She used to be a client for a matchmaking app. The woman is no-nonsense, but I would've thought she'd be against something like this. Was that why she was running away from the guy at the mud run?

"When you say they were matched and it didn't work out, what do you mean? Does the process not work as well as you hoped?" It's a forward question, sure, but I want facts before I commit to anything.

Meg sighs and says, "No, I believe in the program. It essentially matched my husband and I. After a little fake dating stint, of course." There is mischief in her eyes and I lean forward, waiting for the rest of the story.

"Parker was a divorce attorney and I had this business, but I really wanted to start the app. Having no money, I'd reached out to investors, but they wanted proof that my process worked. I figured that the easiest way to do that was to have someone around who could help me out, and vice versa. Parker needed a girlfriend to prove he was ready to become a partner in his father's law firm, but it turned out that I was his match in reality and not just on paper."

I sit back, mulling over the information. "It's interesting that you both used it yourselves."

She nods. "So, I believe in the process, but going global is very different from the way I started this business."

"What all goes into a match?" Kenzie asks.

"Great question," Meg says, standing up. "We'll pop into the next room so I can show you the flow." She grabs what looks to be a walkie-talkie, only a baby version. The baby in the bouncer is sleeping and she looks like a doll.

Meg leaves the room and Kenzie follows. I walk a few steps behind, curious now about this woman who refuses to date yet getting a full walk-through of a matchmaking business.

We're led into a large room with six, large flat-screen TVs mounted on one wall. Each screen has a bunch of information displayed, a few names and characteristics.

Meg turns to us and grins. "We call this the Wall of Love. When I first started out, I did everything by hand and it took quite a while to make a match from the entries. Now the process is streamlined using code that we pull from the intake test, which you've already taken, Kenzie."

Kenzie gives her a curt nod, giving me a sideways glance after. It only multiplies the questions I have in my mind. Mostly, what kind of guy is she into and what happened that made her shut down her account. If she'd been successful at finding a true match, we wouldn't all be standing here.

"Do you have an example of a match? Like, are they similar in a certain percentage of personality traits and interests?" Kenzie's voice shakes just slightly. Is she nervous?

Meg walks over to what looks like a command center with three computer screens and several keyboards. "Okay, let's look you up," she says.

"No, uh, no, I'm good," Kenzie says, her cheeks going red as she looks over and points to me. "I don't need this guy to see all the things. I'd just like a generalized example. When I filled out the intake form, I was working at a marketing firm but now I work as an organizer. Does that change my matches?"

"That's great! I'll need your help in a few weeks once we finish remodeling the next building over," Meg says brightly. "As far as your matches, it shouldn't be too different, but you can retake the test if you're worried about it."

"What are you wanting us to do?" I ask, trying to get to the heart of things. Now that I've seen the impressive operation that goes into the matchmaking process, I'm still not sold on taking part in it.

Meg pulls out a chair for both of us, setting her baby monitor down on the command center. "The TV show has a thriving YouTube channel that gets hundreds of thousands of views worldwide. We've partnered with them to help us film a docuseries on the ins and outs of the matchmaking process. What I would love to have is the two of you enter the pool of candidates and be matched. You'll then film dates with several matches to see how the process goes."

"What if we don't click with our matches?" I ask.

"Or they don't jive with us," Kenzie says, her voice almost inaudible.

"The point of this is to keep going to find that special someone for everyone. We'll reevaluate the matches and see if we've found anything we can fix on our end and then try again."

Kenzie shakes her head. "But isn't that bad publicity for your company if it doesn't work out?"

Meg smiles. "It may hurt my pride a bit, but any publicity is better than none at all. And seeing real life couples with potential matches gives people hope that it will work for them too."

"Understandable." I shift to put my ankle up on the other knee, trying to get comfortable in this very uncomfortable chair. "My agent, Dave, said you had a proposal for me. Is it different for me since I've never been enrolled in your program?"

With a small smile, Meg nods. "There will be at least eight daters who will be matched up. I'll ask that you be willing to film promos and take a few pictures for our marketing efforts. But your teammate thought you'd be a for sure yes."

I frown. "Let me guess. Carson?"

"Carson and Ruby are good friends of mine."

Shaking my head, I say, "I don't know if it would be a good business move to trust him." I laugh, reinforcing the joke.

"He was very serious about the possibility of you helping us out." Meg kept her smile locked on me for several moments before turning a few pages in front of her.

"Okay, so what is it you're proposing? Is there a script we'll have to follow or anything?" My stomach clenches as I'm nervous about whatever it is she's going to say. I almost hope for lines because then I might not choke when the cameras are pointed toward me.

"No script. This will be true filming, awkward moments and all. I'd rather give the truth about what this process is like so others can relate."

"I doubt many people will care about a hockey player in this town."

With a small smile, Meg says, "Don't underscore your worth or my research, Trey. You are one of the fastest rising hockey stars in the NHL right now. Your jersey has been sold more than any other Breeze member to date. Everyone I've reached out to has given you glowing praises. So, I think you'd be perfect to represent our company."

Kenzie shifts, as if she's ready to be out of the room.

"And Kenzie, from what you've shared in your form and what I was able to recover from your account, I think you'd be a great asset for this project. You've been through the matching process and can give a real-life example of trying again." Meg's expression turns pleading and Kenzie squirms more.

Something tugs at me to comfort her in some way, but I've never been good at that kind of thing. My whole life has been all about, "Being tough, staying strong, and don't let the emotions get to you."

"What are the specifics of this? Is there a set number of dates and a time frame for it?" Kenzie asks. For someone who was so gung-ho to avoid dates two days ago, she's giving this some serious thought.

"In a perfect world, I would love to have this work for you in a matter of weeks. If you're up on a billboard talking about our company and then a month later you're at a press conference saying you've found the person you want to spend your life with, I think that would be a pretty great investment." Meg smiles and turns toward the walkie-talkie, as if she had dog-like hearing, because I haven't heard a peep from the baby in the next room. "I think the goal is to have you go on at least four dates with people you've matched with and see where we stand from there."

Could there really be a woman in the computer system that would be okay with my line of work and not just there for the limelight? Someone I could love completely and build a family with?

It's worth a shot.

"Well, I'll give you a tentative yes, pending the contracts," I say. "And nothing can be done during training and games, should this last into the start of the hockey season."

I turn to look at Kenzie, curious about her answer. She notices both sets of eyes staring at her and sighs. "I'm going to need some more time to think about it."

"Understandable. Please let me know if there's anything you need in the meantime."

All three of us stand and walk toward the lobby.

"Oh, I forgot," Meg says. "They've talked about a prize for couples who've found their match, but I'm not sure what that is. A private donor is funding that part, but it's worth giving it your all if you decide to do go for it. Finding a significant other and a cash prize would be worth it, right?"

"If my luck could swing that way, it probably would," Kenzie says dryly.

The monitor crackles and the baby starts crying. "Okay,

team. I've got to run and get SJ, but it was so nice meeting both of you. I hope we get to know each other better over the next few weeks." She smiles and then hurries back into her office.

I turn to study Kenzie's expression and smile when I see she's basically zoned out.

Waving a hand in front of her face, I say, "Anyone home?"

She swats it away and comes back to the present. "Stop. That's exactly what my brothers do." Without saying anything else, she stomps toward the door, and I almost feel the floor shaking in her wake.

Once we're outside, I practically have to jog to keep up with her strides. The woman can move.

"What are you thinking?" I ask, trying to look her in the eyes.

"That I shouldn't have come in at all." Her shoulders slump and she mutters something about, "Trying to be helpful and it backfires."

"What do you have to lose?" I ask, wondering if the question will turn her into a bear that's ready to pounce, or the Kenzie that loosened up on the drive back to my house the other day after the race.

She stops abruptly and I have to backpedal to stand next to her. "You obviously haven't been on the other side of a breakup."

"If you're implying that I don't have much experience when it comes to having a steady girlfriend, you'd be correct." Why did I admit that? I've always prioritized hockey over having a real relationship, but I feel like I'm admitting to being socially challenged with that response.

"Then you're perfect for this. You can gain some experience in Broken Heartsville."

"I take it you dated someone from the app and he broke your heart."

She glares at me, and something about those brown eyes

makes me feel all protective. "I've got to get back to work. See you around."

"What kind of organizing do you do?" I ask after she's taken a few steps away from me. She stops, but doesn't turn around.

"Right now, I'm open to any organizing people need. My current client is a hoarder."

I nod. "Well, I'm not that bad, but you saw the number of boxes in my garage. Any chance you help people unpack and put things where they need to go?"

She nods. "Yeah, I can do that."

"You're hired."

Kenzie works to try and hide the smile on her face, but finally gives in. "You want me to organize your house?"

I shrug. "Yeah, why not?"

"Because you have enough money to hire a real organizer." Something like doubt flashes in her eyes and is gone, leaving the defiant look I'm used to seeing.

"Why pay them when I can pay you? I feel like you'll do a better job with what I want rather than going overboard just to get the paycheck."

"Sounds good. I'll come by tomorrow morning to get a feel for the place and let you know how long it will take."

"Awesome. Thanks, Kenzie. It will be nice to stop living out of boxes and suitcases."

She just shakes her head and waves her hand as she walks by. There is a lot to unpack with her around, but I have a feeling it's going to be worth it.

11

KENZIE

I might be holding onto my bent legs and rocking back and forth on the floor of my closet after that encounter. Sure, my subconscious probably thought I'd see more of Trey once Dani and Miles tied the knot. Even Landon and Rachelle have been hanging out with the group a lot more, so it was inevitable. But to have Trey essentially be my boss?

My mind turns over the entire conversation again and again. I was too rigid right there and should've said something funny. It's no use. I'm not the picture of female grace and personality. It's better people know that I'm prickly from the start.

The conversation with my dad comes to mind again and I think about how I said I'd be willing to work in any aspect of the Breeze club. Does organizing their star wing's home count? Is that fulfilling dreams?

Maybe I'd feel that more once I got to his house.

There's a knock on the door of my room and I say nothing for a few moments. I'm not sure if I want to talk to anyone about anything right now. I'd just accepted to work semi-closely with the guy I need to not think about in a romantic capacity. Ever. My teenage heart would be crushed.

"Kenzie? Are you okay?" Evie's voice calls.

"In here," I say, nudging the closet door open with my foot.

I squint at the stream of light, like I've been trapped in a cave for centuries. Did I just hiss?

"What are you doing in here?" Evie asks, and standing behind her and I can see a faint glimmer of red hair in the back there. Dani comes into view, and I'm surprised to see her there, since she moved out once she got married. It isn't until Hillary pushes the others aside and sits down half-in and half-outside the closet that I laugh, long and loud.

"Is she going to be okay?" Evie asks, her attention directed at Hillary.

Hillary pushes me a bit and nods. "Yeah, she'll be fine. I'd say she either quit another job or had a steamy encounter with a certain hockey player." She grins at me, and I end up sticking my tongue out at her. The others visibly relax. They're still getting used to the girl who's been one of my best friends since junior year of high school.

"Is that a poster of Trey on your wall?" Millie asks, pointing inside my closet.

I scramble to my feet, doing everything I can to hide the poster with my arms spread out and my body covering a large photo of him in his hockey gear. Except his head is still visible over mine. I've managed to keep my feelings for him a secret over the past six months since I moved in, but it looks like I've finally been caught.

"Yes, it's a poster of Trey." I might as well own the truth.

"I take it Kenzie hasn't filled you in on the extent of her knowledge of Trey Hatch?" Hillary says. She stands and the others all find a spot around the room to sit down, as if ready for all the tea. "They used to go to hockey camps together. She's known him since before he was famous. And can quote just about every stat you need to know about his hockey career."

I avoid looking up, knowing each of them are looking at me like I'm some sort of psycho. I don't actively stalk the guy. Okay, online doesn't count.

"That's definitely new information," Dani says, laughing. "I suspected there were feelings there, which puts into perspective the situation after the Breeze game. And why you didn't want to drive him home after the race."

"Does he remember you?" Millie asks, perched on the corner of my bed. She's flashing a dreamy expression, like I'm on the tip of landing a date with my long-time crush.

With a long shake of my head, something pulls loose in my chest. "No. Not even a hint. I haven't really mentioned my time at the rink or anything. He was at Love, Austen today when I went there to pick up–"

"I'm sorry, did you just say you went to Love, Austen?" Dani asks.

I nod, wondering how I can worm my way out of this story. But my mind is so muddled I kind of want to tell them. So, I explain the survey and how I wanted to give Meg some more insight into how to help people avoid situations like mine.

"You have to do it," Millie says, looking more determined than I've ever seen her.

"I don't think I can. I mean, go on dates with people and have it filmed for the world to see? It's too much."

Evie takes a seat next to Hillary. "But if Trey is in the running, isn't that a good sign? Maybe the two of you will be matched." There's a giddy sigh that floats through the room and I shake my head.

"I'm cursed. And now that Dani is married into the friend group, if I screw anything up, I'll have to move to some foreign country and never talk about my former life again."

"Oh, come on," Hillary says, "You sound more dramatic than me, and that's saying something."

"Trey waited for you and helped you throughout the mud run," Evie says, grinning. "That's got to count for something."

Millie sighs and says, "That's so romantic. He's like your knight in shining armor."

Raising my pointer finger, I shake it along with my head. "No, no, not going to happen. There's not even a chance of me being his damsel in distress. I was the one who had to drag him out of the water to make sure he didn't drown."

"To be fair, you didn't look like this when you knew him," Hillary says, waving her arm up and down in front of me.

Cue the blushing, and I'm not even close to Trey.

"Do you have a picture of you when you would've met him the first time?" Evie asks.

Dani nods. "Yeah, that would be fun to see."

I bite my lip, trying to decide if it's worth it to my pride to show them the book of hockey stuff I've kept over the years. And how much I really have changed since.

I stand and walk over to my dresser, pulling out the bottom drawer.

"Is that bejeweled?" Hillary says, walking over to check out the cover. "Even I've never seen this thing."

"That's because you got all funny when you went to college and started dating Roy."

Hillary nods in acknowledgement. "True. Sorry about that —about everything."

I hope that means she's sorry about ditching her own wedding and not telling me about it, or going no-contact for several months. We'll have to hash that out more later.

I nod and focus on the pages, finding the one I've stared at way too many times. A group picture of the last year Trey attended the camp. He looks like a younger version of his handsome self while I, well, let's just say I was the late-bloomer to his right.

After letting out a deep breath, I hand over the book to Evie and the rest of them crowd around, oohing and ahhing as they take in the picture.

"Look at all these little hockey skaters," Evie says with a big grin. "There's Trey."

I pause, wondering how long it will take them to find me. Seconds tick past and it's like they all come to the realization at the same time.

"I don't see you, Kenz," Dani says, leaning in closer as if that will help find me in the somewhat grainy picture.

"I'm right next to Trey. On the right." I turn around, not wanting to see their reactions to this news.

Silence.

"Wait, that's you?" Millie asks, her disbelief thick.

I can see them through the mirror on top of my dresser. It's like they're trying to reconcile the differences from that picture taken ten years ago.

With a nod, I say, "Yep. The chubby girl with braces and the ridiculous set of bangs. Welcome to my never-ending awkward teen years."

"They definitely ended, Kenz," Hillary said.

"Thanks to you. I wouldn't know anything about makeup or style really if you hadn't randomly befriended me." My mother tried to get me to dress a certain way, but it was the subtle changes Hillary suggested that actually hit home.

Hillary laughs. "Randomly? It was more like I needed to pass Algebra 2 and knew you were good at math enough to help me not flunk out."

Millie claps her hands together. "Okay, so did you do some kind of makeover to try and get the guy of your dreams to take you to prom?"

I laugh and say, "As much as I would love it to be, my life

has been far from a rom com movie plot. Hillary just helped me figure out a few of the basic style tips before we graduated. I entered college as a not-so-plain athlete."

"You are anything but plain. Your cheekbones are perfect," Evie says and shakes her head. "So, what was your relationship with Trey like at these camps?"

I walk over and sink into the small bean bag chair I've had since college. "Let's be honest, I was the cocky girl doing what I could to beat all the boys. Trey was chill, but I doubt he ever gave me a second thought. As evidenced by the fact he hasn't said anything since we've reconnected. Or whatever you call it."

"Did you like him back then?"

I close my eyes and nod. "He was the one I always pictured as my future boyfriend. I compared everyone to him, at least until I started dating Donovan." My lips pinch shut, not ready to let anything else out. Donovan, the real guy who I thought would be my forever.

"Donovan?" Dani asks. The other two lean in and even Hillary is interested.

"Let's talk about that some other time," I say, standing and taking the book back. I secure it in the bottom drawer before I turn back to my housemates.

"Check out Kenzie being all mysterious and stuff," Evie says with a grin.

"Well, at least you'll be working with Trey," Dani says, something mischievous in her eyes.

"No, don't you dare. I don't need anyone leaking this to him or to any of the guys. You especially, Dani. Miles does not need to know." I was always taught not to point fingers, but I'm hoping that she'll get the point.

Dani sighs. "I just gave my vows a few weeks ago to be honest with each other. How can–"

"You can be honest without spilling your guts about this," I say, my hand beginning to shake. That's all I need is to have

Trey remember the awkward chubby girl from hockey camp and then be weirded out every time he sees me. "I don't think he'll be bringing up topics where we have any connection."

After several long moments, Dani nods. "Okay, I'll do my best. But if this blows up in my face, I'm blaming you for it."

"It won't. Because no one needs to act any differently when he comes around, all right?" I focus on each of them, one at a time to get their confirmation.

I sink to the floor, all the stress of the past hour taking the energy from my muscles.

"How about a movie night? We can order in Chinese and eat chocolate."

A sniffle escapes me. "I think I'm out."

Every head turns to me in surprise.

"I mean, I'm out of chocolate. How can a girl turn down Chinese and a chick flick?"

"We can order that too. Kenzie without chocolate isn't something I want to see," Hillary says. "I might even run out to the store to get some."

I laugh and stand, ready to do anything to get my brain off the events of tonight. I'd be lucky to get through organizing Trey's home without someone spilling the beans.

"Just so you know, I was over him a long time ago. So please don't be weird."

"We won't," Millie says. She's the one I'm most worried about.

"I'm calling bull," Dani says, her hands on her hips as she stands in the doorway. "There's no way you don't have feelings for the guy after the posters in your closet, your crazy knowledge of all his stats, and how you act every time he's around."

I open my mouth to refute it, but it would be a lie. "Okay, so I'm still working on it. Closer each day. Don't you live with your husband now?"

Dani gives me another look that tells me she doesn't believe it. "Yes, but he's out with the guys and I needed a girl's night."

"We'll keep you then," I say, smiling at her.

Her phone rings and she says, "But it looks like he forgot something. I'll be right back." She disappears down the stairs.

"We might as well get popcorn going," I say. Takeout will be at least another thirty minutes and after all the stress of today, I'm going to need something to snack on.

"I still think you should do the docuseries," Evie says, grabbing a blanket from the back of the couch and wrapping it around herself.

"Why?" I say, thinking she's joking.

"Look at the perks. You'll get to date people who you'd be compatible with. There's also the chance one of them could be Trey. And you'll get a cash prize if it works out. I know I wouldn't turn down a little extra cash."

I close my eyes for a moment, trying to register her words. "Maybe I'll put your name up for the vote," I say, grinning at her.

She shakes her head. "Don't you dare. I'll be in charge of the popcorn when these episodes air."

As the others banter about what movie we should watch, I let myself imagine what it would be like to actually be Trey's girlfriend. And then I shut down that sentiment quickly. Based on my research, I'm not his type.

12

TREY

"Turn around." Miles and I are in my car on our way to a reunion dinner for Owen, who came back from his medical mission trip. We're not even three blocks from Miles' house when he's directing me past the road that leads to the restaurant.

"Where are we going?" I ask, confused.

He's already got his phone up to his ear and is grinning like a fool when I hear Dani's voice on the other end. "Yeah, I forgot to give you the keys to the car. We'll drop them off on our way to dinner. Meet me outside?"

I frown, trying to reconcile the man before me with the Miles I used to know. Granted, he didn't come from the easiest of family backgrounds, but it's like Dani has turned him into a warm tub of butter.

"Keys? Why does she need the keys?"

He gives me a half-smile and says, "She managed to lose her keys to the house and we haven't had a chance to get a copy made yet. I don't want her locked out if she gets home before us."

"You are the ultimate example, bruh," I say, laughing when my attempt at a lower octave backfires.

We'd all done a bunch of shuffling over the past few months, me getting a new house, Miles gaining a wife. Jack's vet clinic now takes on large animals as well as the small variety, and Spencer has been holed up in his house working on the audiobook jobs he's getting from a bunch of indie authors. I'll catch up with Owen tonight, but I'm excited to hang out in a less muddy environment with all of them.

The drive isn't too far away and I pull up to a small house. The front lawn is covered in blow-up pool animals. Not the small ones, but the giant ones that could be used on a lake.

"What happened?" I ask, waving to the yard.

"Dani says it's a bet between Evie and the next-door neighbor. There's something crazy every time we stop by."

I still don't know all of Dani's former roommates that well. I'd been in the postseason when Miles and Dani's romance took off, which means I didn't get in on all the jokes Spencer and Jack did. At least Owen is in the same boat I am.

Miles disappears inside and I wait for a couple minutes. And then the impatience hits.

I practically run to the door and knock, hoping we can get going. We're supposed to be at the restaurant in ten minutes and it's going to take almost twenty to get there.

The door opens and instead of Dani and Miles, Kenzie is behind it.

"Why are you here?" she asks, studying me. And then her gaze moves behind me and her eyes go wide as she sees the blowups.

She waves me in and takes a step back. "Evie!" she calls up the stairs.

I'm not sure where to stand so I stay near the front door, hoping Miles will come down and save me.

A girl with short brown hair walks down the stairs. "I think

I found one of your bars of chocolate, Kenz." She's waving an extra-large Hershey's in the air.

I open my mouth to ask a question, but Kenzie speaks first. "Have you seen what the neighbor did now? The guy might break a hip trying to outdo you."

Evie walks over and glances out the door, a soft laugh escaping her. In seconds, the sound is loud and deep, making me follow suit.

"Your neighbor does that?" I direct the question to Kenzie because Evie looks like she won't be able to form a coherent sentence.

Kenzie folds her arms across her chest and gives me a curt nod. "They started this war a couple weeks ago. I'm not sure how the man does it because he's got to be in his eighties." She shakes her head and walks into the kitchen, pulling out a bag of popcorn. The smell reaches me quickly. It's probably black in spots.

"Did you need something?" she asks, throwing the bag into the garbage can. She glances at me in between opening the package of a new bag of popcorn and placing it back into the microwave.

"Yeah, I came to find Miles. He said he was just dropping off the keys to Dani so we could go."

"Good luck. Dani said she needed to show him something upstairs. I doubt they'll be down soon. They've been taken by the *Black Hole*."

I've never heard that before, except for the small units on space throughout my public education. "The what?"

Kenzie is combing through the fridge now, pulling out packages and sniffing them before emptying them into the sink. I walk a few steps closer. Is she cleaning out the fridge while waiting for popcorn to cook?

"Sorry," she says, spraying the contents down the disposal. "It's something we used to joke about when my brother,

Damian, got married. It's like they have no concept of anyone else around them. Once the vows are said the PDA is through the roof."

I'd never thought of it like that, but now that she's talking about it, I see what she means. "How long are they usually in this *Black Hole*?"

"It ranges. Anywhere from three months to life."

Laughing, I say, "That sounds a lot like a jail sentence."

She shrugs. "Close enough."

"Have you given some thought to the whole match film thing?"

She turns off the water and then grabs a towel, drying off her hands. After she's folded it and set it back on the counter, she looks to me. If this is how thorough she is on regular things, I definitely hired the right woman to organize my place.

"The ref is still looking at the tape to see what the right call is."

What is it about this woman that makes me want to stay a while? Not tonight, obviously, but she is quirky in the best way.

"So, you're saying there's a chance?" I say, grinning.

She raises an eyebrow. "You want me to be part of it that badly? We'll be going on dates with other people."

"I don't know, I feel like we could be the dream team. Maybe we can request double dates."

"Again, I'm not sold on the idea."

"Maybe I can help with that."

Her eyes go wide and she takes a step back. The microwave beeps and she turns as if that was the plan all along.

"Are you ready to go?" Miles asks. His face is all red and I'm thinking there might be the start of a hickey along his collar.

Shaking my head, I say, "The real question is if you're ready. I think your assessment is correct, Dr. Kenzie." I give her a wink and smile when her cheeks flush.

"Right about what?" Miles asks, walking toward the front door.

"It's an inside joke. You had to be there."

At the front door I hesitate. What would it be like to blow off the guys and hang out with Kenzie? She obviously has knowledge of hockey and is always one step ahead of me when it comes to humor. But I'll see her tomorrow when she walks through my house.

I make a mental note to get home early enough to pick up a bit. I don't need Kenzie to think I'm a slob. But I do need time to convince her to join the dating pool. The question is what would make her crack?

13

TREY

"What's the story with Kenzie?" I ask Miles in the car as we drive to the restaurant. For the first time in a long while, I'm not frustrated by the tardiness.

Miles turns to look at me. "What do you mean?"

"She's really funny. I don't know much about her and I'm curious."

With a wide grin, Miles says, "Really? I can see something happening between you two."

Shaking my head, I blow out a breath. "No, not like that. I hired her to organize my house and while I think she'll do a good job of it, I know all of two things about her. She likes hockey and she's funny. I'm just doing my due diligence." Yeah, I'll try to convince myself of that.

"She doesn't just like hockey. She loves it. You should've seen her in the box at your game, man. I want to say she played in college or something."

While that's news to me, I can see it. "Do you know where?"

Miles shrugs. "Somewhere in the city, from what Dani told me. And as far as organizing, she's probably the best one for it. I might hire her just to come organize our house after Dani finally gets all her stuff moved in. It's a good thing you hired Kenzie, though. I can't believe you've lived in your house this long and the place looks the same as the day you moved in. I'm willing to bet you don't have your TV plugged in yet."

I grit my teeth. "I'm not taking that bet." It's true, the TV is still in the box. When it comes to home improvement tasks, even something as small as hooking up the TV, I'm all thumbs.

My mind is still trying to puzzle through Kenzie's personality as we walk into the restaurant.

"What time did you all get here?" I ask, taking a seat next to Jack and across from Owen.

"Twenty minutes ago, man. We thought you might've fallen asleep or decided on a dinner date with the flavor of the week," Jack says, grinning.

I punch him in the shoulder hard enough to make him sway into Spencer. "Please. I've never been like that. I'd say you and Spencer have that title locked down," I say, directing my response to Jack. "The reason we're late is because of Lover Boy over here."

Miles grins and nods. "I'm okay with that."

"I'm gone a whole month and come back to the same bickering from you two," Owen says with a laugh.

"How was the trip?" I ask, hoping the waitress comes soon so I can order a drink.

Owen nods and grins. He's one of the top nurses in the area and even talked about becoming a travel nurse at one point. "It was awesome. The perfect break to the rat race I've had here. Guatemala has some amazing people and is beautiful. We were able to help so many in need. On the few days off we had, we toured some of the areas and it's incredible. I already signed up to go on to the next one."

"Which is when?" Miles asks from the other side of him.

"I think in about six months. What's new with the rest of you?"

Jack shakes his head. "My life is a zoo man."

We all laugh, even though Jack, as a vet, has used that joke countless times since he finished vet school.

"I've got several books I'm set to narrate," Spencer says, holding up his Coke. "And I've even got a callback for an animated film."

Spencer grew up as a child actor, starring in several popular TV series and a couple of movies. As he grew, he'd done more of the back scene stuff, taking on various voice acting jobs. The last time we'd had a good serious talk, he wanted to start producing, and from everything he's done before, I think he'd be great at it.

"Well, Dani and I are almost moved into the house," Miles says with a chuckle. "She insists we don't get a moving van to move her stuff and we just keep making trips back and forth in my car. I'm about ready to just hire a company to get whatever's left."

"She didn't grow up like you did, Miles," Jack says with a somber smile.

Miles raises his hands and says, "I know. We've learned a lot more about each other since the wedding. But I love her in spite of her quirks."

"And she tolerates yours," Owen says with a laugh. He turns to me and asks, "What's new with you? How's the off-season going?"

It takes me a moment to focus since Miles's words are still running over and over in my brain. "It's going. Just trying to stay in shape. I've hired Dani's old roommate, Kenzie, to organize my house for me and–"

"Good idea," Spencer says, nodding.

I lean forward to focus on him. "What do you mean?" I say, laughing.

"Dude, I lived with you for two years in college. I'm surprised the stench of hockey body odor hasn't been burned into my nostrils. And you need help with where to put all the little things instead of just leaving them in a pile on the counter."

We all laugh at that. I think about the other thing I want to share—if I should go through with the docuseries or not. I trust their opinion.

"And Dave set me up to be part of a local company." I'm a chicken, so that's all I say as I prep for a better explanation.

"Which one?" Jack asks, twisting the paper from his straw around his finger.

I blow out a breath and say, "Love, Austen. They're a–"

"Matchmaking company!" Miles says, leaning on the table so hard that the table tilts, causing some of the drinks to slide toward him. He misses his own but catches Owen's Sprite. We all pass down our napkins like this is a normal occurrence.

The other three sets of eyes focus on me while Miles mops up the mess.

"You're going to work for a matchmaking company?" Spencer asks.

"They know your track record with women, right?" Owen says with a grin.

I throw a napkin his way but it doesn't make it that far. "I don't have a track record. I have a list of women who want to be with me for fame and the jewels I can buy with my salary. Another category would be the women my mother has given my number to and/or invited to dinner."

Jack shakes his head. "Out of the hundred women–"

"More like fifty," I correct.

"—you've dated in the past year, not one was willing to stick around to take home to Mama Hatch?"

I grimace. "I took Candice home. That was a mistake."

Candice and I met at a gala her family had put on for one of the charities in Boston around six months ago. Things had gone so well that we'd gone on dates or hung out every day for the following two weeks. It was fast, but it felt right to have her meet the family. I wouldn't have proposed that quickly, but it was nice to have my mom off my back for all of five days, knowing that I was in a relationship.

My parents live in a middle-class neighborhood in a house they've worked for years to fix up. It's the nicest house on the block and I'm always proud to show off the skills I learned alongside my dad. Sure, I didn't do much of the cutting of boards or anything, but those memories are of the only other skills I have besides professional hockey.

Candice was not impressed with my family's social status and then she ghosted me.

There is a collective silence in the room. "Not everyone is going to care that your family isn't worth millions," Spencer says, breaking the tension.

"Well, maybe this is the way to do it. Maybe using a matchmaker is the only way I can find someone who will look past my career and see me." The words are raw, something I didn't realize I needed to say until they were out.

"What are the terms?" Owen asks, picking up a fork to start on his eggs the waitress sets down in front of him.

"It's a docuseries on the process of matchmaking. I'll have to fill out the test that helps match the couples and then go on several dates while they film it all."

"Send me the contract before you sign anything," Miles says. "I'll look at them for you and make sure you're not bound to marry any of them. Unless you want to, that is."

"Thanks, man," I say, settling back into my seat.

Jack snorts. "Isn't that Dave's job?"

Shaking my head, I say, "Dave is great for a lot of things, but the fine print is not his specialty."

"I could do a better job than that guy does," Spencer says. "I still have so many contacts from my acting days."

"What are you talking about?" Owen says, laughing. "I thought you were still acting."

"Not as much anymore. I'm kind of liking this work-from-home setup I have going." Spencer leans back in his chair and grins.

The waitress brings out the rest of the food and I smile when she sets down the meatlover's omelet. The guys must've ordered it for me since that's my go-to meal whenever we hit a diner.

Once we finish dinner, we all walk out, chatting in smaller groups. Owen slaps me on the back and says, "I missed you, man. I'm glad you made it out tonight."

"I haven't been gone that much. You know how the post-season gets."

"Well, not personally, as every time I try to skate on the ice I end up face planting. But I'll take your word for it." Owen laughs at what is probably a surprised expression on my face. He's always been good at pointing out the literal stuff.

"Right," I say, shaking my head.

"What are you feeling about the whole matchmaking thing? Do you think you'll do it?"

With a shrug, I say, "I think so. I mean, seeing Miles and Dani these past few months has been good, but hard, like, after all I've accomplished in my life, I'm still missing something."

"A girl isn't going to solve all your problems, Trey," he says, giving me a nudge in the shoulder with his fist.

"Tell me that when Riley dumps you," I say, thinking of his long-time girlfriend. She's also in the nursing profession and they might even be worse than Miles and Dani in the PDA department.

Owen stuffs his hands into his pockets and glances down at the ground. "Actually, she broke up with me the night I got home. Something about having space gave her time to think about our relationship."

I blink several times, feeling like a cartoon character blindsided by a shocking revelation. And this is definitely shocking.

"Why didn't you say anything about it when we were in there?" I ask, gesturing toward the door.

"I'm still processing it. It's been two days and I still can't get her words out of my brain. I've analyzed every inch of our relationship and still can't figure out what went wrong."

The man looks like he's being held up by a couple of sticks and a strong wind will blow him over.

I lean in for a bro-hug and say, "I'm sorry, man. I thought you two were going to make it."

"Me too. I picked out a ring and everything."

I throw my hands in the air. "When were you going to tell me?"

"When I needed your help to come up with an amazing proposal. But that will have to wait for now."

"So, what about your job? I mean, don't you two work the same shifts?"

Owen's lips press into a fine line. "Yeah, well, it seems she asked to be switched to another shift and department. And several of the other nurses were talking about it when I walked by. Apparently, she's dating one of the attending doctors now."

That's what the look is. Unadulterated heartbreak from a blindsided break up. "I can't believe she moved on while you were gone for a month. How long were the two of you together?"

"Three years this November. We might need to have some more guys' nights out, maybe venture into some clubs when all the anniversaries crop up."

I slap him on the back. "I'm here for you man. As much as possible. Maybe we can have some daytime drinks when we're in season."

Owen laughs and nods. "I'd say, if you haven't made up your mind, go for the docuseries thing. If it works out, I might even sign up." We laugh and the rest of the group joins in.

"Sign up for what?" Spencer asks.

"For the matchmaking program," Owen says. That makes everyone question what's going on and he gives them a brief explanation that he's the newest single guy on the market.

Jack waves his finger back and forth and says, "Yes, please sign up. There won't be a lady in Boston who will look at me and Spence with you available."

Owen shakes his head, laughing at the comment. "I doubt that. Most women think a male nurse is weird and getting past that takes a while." He glances down at his watch and says, "I better get going. I'm on the night shift tonight in the ER."

He waves goodbye and heads down the sidewalk to the train.

"I never thought I'd see the day when he and Riley weren't together," Spencer says.

"Yeah, I thought he'd be the first one of the group to get married," I say, nudging Miles.

With a shrug, Miles grins. "Sometimes love happens when you least expect it."

Jack groans. "That's the worst cliche I've ever heard. Are we up for some games? I've got a few new ones since we last played."

"Nope," Miles says. "I'm sticky in places I don't want to think about and I miss my wife."

Spence, Jack, and I gag and Miles laughs. "You wish you could say the same."

As much as I don't want to admit it, that's exactly what I want. Not the sticky part, just the wife.

14

TREY

After dropping Miles off at his house, I stayed up extra late playing cards at Jack's and got a hangover from the lack of sleep, and a couple drinks. What can I say? It's hard to want to go home to an empty house. Maybe that's why I haven't put everything away yet, either. I'd rather hire someone else to do it than wonder what a future spouse would say about the state of my house.

That and my mother's constant nagging about how I need to find a wife and give her grandbabies only adds to the headache from the few drinks I had.

And then the sun is shining through the windows and I realize I missed my alarm. The morning workout I'd planned would have to wait until later, at least until after Kenzie arrives.

I walk out, grabbing a protein shake to get started and then hurry to pick up some of the clothes I'd left out the past few days. If Kenzie is a cleaning fanatic, as I suspect, this might have her running for the hills.

When I lean over to pick up my dirty socks that are partially hidden by the couch, I can smell the body odor mixed with deodorant on my t-shirt. Not pleasant.

I strip it off and hurry into the laundry room to drop it in the laundry basket. I'm trying to find something clean, but no luck here. My bedroom is the next spot and I search for something fresh in the several open boxes strewn around the room. Has it really been that long since I last did laundry?

The doorbell rings as I'm no closer to finding something not covered in dried sweat. I pause. Do I just answer the door and then hurry back to my room and get a shirt? Do I even have a t-shirt presentable for someone to come over?

"Come in," I say, making sure my voice is loud enough to hear through the living room and to the door.

There's a pause and then a muffled, "It's locked."

Right. My father had drilled into me the importance of locking up. He'd always circled the house at least four times every night to make sure everything was secure. Even during the day, it seemed like we never unlocked things unless we re-locked them right away.

There's nothing. I'm out of t-shirts.

Kenzie knocks again and I dart out, looking for any shirts I might've dropped somewhere discreet in my time relaxing in my own home.

I decide to grab the blanket off the couch and wrap it around myself. Why am I being weird about this? It's not like I'm into flaunting my pecs and abs around, but for some reason, this just isn't the time and place to test that. Kenzie is helping me out with something and she doesn't need a sideshow.

Pulling the door open, Kenzie is standing outside, a large bag over one shoulder and a steel mug in her hand.

"Good morning. You're on time," I say.

She raises her watch to about two inches from my face and says, "Early. Did I wake you?" She gives me an up-and-down glance, her gaze stopping around my upper chest area where the blanket doesn't cover. "I don't know why I didn't take you for a blanket guy."

"What does that mean?" Has she been thinking about me? Hopefully I haven't hired some stalker girl who will never leave me alone after the job is finished.

She doesn't really give off those types of vibes though.

Kenzie walks inside the house and does a small turn, her gaze roaming the room. "I mean, the guys I've dated never broke down and used blankets. An ex told me he didn't feel manly using a blanket."

"So, no blankets at night? None when he's sick or when he's cuddling up to watch a movie?" She shakes her head and I make a funny face, which gets her to laugh. I like the sound of it and it makes me want to recreate it. "Well, yeah, then I can't relate. I have to have a blanket when I'm watching a movie."

"What about the movie theater? Are you Linus, hauling a blankie everywhere?"

I laugh and say, "Now that you mention it, I might have to try that next time I go to a movie." I hold up the corners of the blanket and say, "This one might be a little hot in the summer though."

Her gaze drops down to my abs and her cheeks turn a rosy shade. And in a moment of self-conscious reflection, I wrap the blanket back around me. Even though Kenzie is cute, I'm not awake enough to enjoy being ogled.

The tops of her ears turn pink and she shakes her head. "I don't know, maybe an afghan type guy." There's a hint of a smile playing at the corners of her lips and I feign hurt at that.

"You mean the scratchy blankets with holes? My grandmother made those for all her grandchildren and great-grandchildren. I think it's still in a bag at my mom's so I won't ruin it with all my moving. Or in a box in the guest bedroom. They're not the best blankets though because they always let in the air."

"Right?" Kenzie says and we both just awkwardly stare at each other for a few seconds. "So, um, do you want to show me what you need from me? Or do you need me to go get a caffeine drip for you to wake up first?"

Funny. "I'm good. Let me just go put this blanket back and we'll get started." I hurry to my room, hoping that there is a decent shirt stuck in the boxes that I overlooked before. There's one in the bathroom and it's still folded neatly. Just another example of why I need organizational help.

I pull a black t-shirt over my head and walk out into the living room. It isn't until the shirt is fully on that I realize it's a cropped version of the ones my sister, Payton, likes to wear. The Breeze logo takes up most of the front but there is enough air hitting my stomach that I know this wasn't the right move.

"Did you lose half your shirt?" Kenzie asks. "Or is that your girlfriend's?"

Something about her comment makes me curious. Is she fishing for information?

"This must be my sister's. She likes to modify all the shirts I pass along and she must've left it in the box when I moved here. Then again, I remember you sporting a similar look a few days ago at the mud race." I wink at her and instead of getting the big smile I'm used to seeing from other women, Kenzie's eyes go wide and she turns to study the fireplace on the far wall.

"How long have you been here?" Kenzie asks.

"About a month."

She turns and narrows her gaze at me. Her pointer finger is aimed at the television box I've had sitting against a table since moving in. "You've been here that long and haven't hooked up the TV?"

I shrug. "Yeah, well, I've been busy and just haven't gotten around to it, a lot like the rest of the house. The only thing I've put together is the gym space over here." I wave for her to follow and point out the kitchen, guest bathroom, guest bedroom, and the office before we get to the gym.

She nods. "Wow, this is an impressive in-home setup."

"Do you lift?"

"A couple times a week."

Again with the awkward silence. "Cool, cool," I say, trying to keep things going. I've never had this hard of a time talking to a woman before. Not that I'm trying to flirt or anything, I guess I'm just intrigued by the fact she's not begging me to be her boyfriend.

Kenzie pulls out a notebook from her bag. "Okay, let's go room by room and you can tell me what it is you want there. If you don't care, I can give you some ideas and see what you think."

I nod, grateful that not all the pressure will be on me for this. We turn and head back toward my bedroom, standing in the doorway. "All I have is my bed in here. A large dresser would be nice. I gave mine to my younger sister when I moved."

She starts scribbling something on the notebook and says, "I have some ideas of what could go with the bed. I'm not really an interior designer, but I can give you some options on what could work, and we can find something that's your style."

Not that I know what my style is. Aside from the mint blue and navy blue colors from being on the Breeze, I don't really have a style. "That would be great. I've never really had a place this big to worry about decorating."

Kenzie laughs. "Where did you live before this?"

"A bunch of my college teammates had a house downtown. It took a while to save up because I have to pay my agent and publicist and all the other people that help with life off the ice. I wanted to have a good amount saved up before I branched out to a place like this."

"Well, you definitely picked a great spot. Is it weird living by yourself now?" Her expression is thoughtful, which contrasts with the word 'weird.'

I chuckle and nod. "Yeah, I mean, it's nice to not get woken up in the middle of the night during a drunken tirade by one of the guys. None of them went on to play hockey after college and most hadn't understood that people still have to function the next morning. I don't need much, but I do need sleep."

Her cheeks turn a rosy color. She spins and walks toward the guest bedroom. "I'm guessing you're going to need a little of everything in here?" She pushes open the door and her posture changes.

I step up next to her, hoping she won't back out on me now. "Yeah, so, um, my mom keeps just about everything I've ever touched. Let's just say my dad was excited when I bought this house."

Boxes line every part of the room, except for one small walkway to get into it. "Um, that seems a bit extreme." Kenzie opens one of the boxes and I peek over her shoulder, seeing only a mess of papers and awards from my elementary days.

I chuckle and nod. "Yeah. She'll probably need help next, after you're done here, I mean."

She blinks a few times but hasn't moved since she opened the box. I wave a hand in front of her face and she swats it away with the notebook.

"Sorry, I just wanted to make sure you're okay."

Kenzie swallows and nods. "This will be fine. It's better that it doesn't come with goop or cockroaches."

I cringe. "Yeah, my home is cockroach free and I hope to keep it that way."

She gives me a small smile. "I'm not going to come plant cockroach eggs here, if that's what you're thinking."

I press my hand to my chest. "Thank you for that. I mean, I didn't think I'd have to worry about that on the walk-thru of my home, but hey, this is all new to me." There's a long pause and I start scrubbing at my arms as if the cockroaches are here now.

"Are you okay?" Kenzie asks, giving me a side glare.

"I'm great," I say, dropping my hands to the sides.

"What's your vision for this room? A guest room? An office?"

"Yeah. Make it comfortable for whoever comes to stay." Not that I have a list of people I'm ready to host right now. Life is crazy enough as it is with the long season and then my trainings to stay in top shape. "I guess if any of my friends from past teams come visit. I can't think of anyone else right now."

Kenzie's soft smile at that answer makes me wonder if I passed some sort of unasked question or test.

We go through the rest of the house and I'm surprised by how thorough she is. "Are you sure you haven't worked with a ton of people before? You're more professional than my real estate agent was when showing me houses."

"I'll take that as a compliment," she says with a little laugh. "I actually just did this with my dad the other day. Well, not exactly this conversation. He's got a lot more junk to work with than you do."

"What do you think? Are you in?"

Kenzie shrugs. "This is a no-brainer, although with that pile of boxes, I can't promise I'll be in and out in three days. If they're all filled with papers, it could be a while. But I can come back when I've got things arranged in my calendar."

For some strange reason, I'm a little sad about that. She's been a puzzle for sure, but I was hoping to have stuff moving along before the docuseries starts. I'm more curious about her every time she comes around. It's like she's got this hard outer shell. But crack her open a bit and her personality is snarky and fun. "I'm in and out of negotiations with it being the off-season. Let me know when you'll be over and I'll make sure to get here."

She frowns at me, a flicker of worry in her eyes. "You don't have to be here for the whole process. That's why you hired me, right?"

"Right," I say, thinking that through. "What's your hourly rate? And do you have some sort of contract we need to sign?"

Her eyes go wide and she says, "Um, great question. I hadn't really gotten that far yet."

"Okay, well, let me know. Whatever you need, I'll pay it."

She laughs and shakes her head. "You must not have to negotiate a whole lot."

I glance around the room for a moment, trying to remember the last time I had to do that. "Not really. That's what Dave is for. And my mom before that. But I know what it's like trying to get started in business. My dad was a framer for residential homes and there were always people trying to get things cheaper. A good day of work is worth whatever it costs at this point."

Silence hits as she narrows her eyes at me, as if trying to put together some invisible puzzle. And then the mask flies back up and she snaps back to reality. "Okay, I'll get you some numbers and a contract as soon as I can." She turns toward the door and I glance out the window at the driveway and along the curb.

"Sounds good. Do you need a ride somewhere?" My house isn't the most accessible to the local trains and buses.

"No, I should be good. It will help me get my steps in today," she says with a smile. I watch her walk down the few steps to my porch and again that sense I should know her hits me.

"Did you decide on the Love, Austen thing?" I ask, stepping out onto the concrete step. The wind blows against my shirt and I remember again that I'm not wearing enough material for anyone to be comfortable.

She shakes her head. "You heard me adamantly say no dating at the mud race. Right? Yep, I'm pretty sure you were there for that. That's a hard pass."

"I don't want to be on camera either," I say, giving her a small smile.

She turns away. "Don't look at me like that. I'm not getting dragged into your dating problems. And there's no way anyone is going to want to date me."

"Come on, Kenz. You're fun and a lot of guys would love the chance to go out with a gal like you."

She waves to the empty sidewalk. "Check the line of people who agree with you. I'm not putting myself through that kind of torture."

"What if I make you a deal?"

I'm not sure why I'm pushing so hard to get her to go along with the docuseries, but maybe it's the idea that everyone should be able to find love. And if Kenzie can find it as jaded as she is, maybe there's hope for me.

15

KENZIE

This whole situation is surreal. I've just walked through Trey's home as my second official job of my business. He's standing here on the sidewalk, barefoot and wearing a crop top of a Breeze t-shirt, asking to make me a deal to go on a dating documentary.

Why does the sound of that make me want to abandon my plan of staying single for the rest of my life and follow this Pied Piper to my death?

"What kind of deal?" I ask, trying to keep my face impassive. A poker face has never been a strong suit, but I'm working with what I've got for now.

"If you agree to do it, I'll owe you big. What if you came out on the ice for one of the games?" He frowns, like he isn't sure what that would do.

"You'll let me skate with your team?" My heart is pumping a million times faster than normal.

"I mean, if you like that. Do you skate?"

I scowl and say, "Of course. I might even skate circles around you now." Closing my mouth, I hope he doesn't catch onto that last word. "Skating on the Breeze home ice would be a dream come true. But I don't think it would be the same value as suffering through dates and being filmed."

Trey pauses a moment. "You like games, right?"

I laugh and nod. "Is Carson Carver the best center in the league? Of course!"

He looks defeated by that. "You really think he's the best? What about yours truly?"

I shake my head, not falling for that. "Trey, you are the perfect wing. I don't know why your coach keeps putting you as the center. Your abilities are better from the sides."

He seems to think about that for a moment. "I guess I'll take that as a compliment, from a knowledgeable source."

And there it is. I've just been friend zoned. Whenever a guy has agreed with me on a sports matter, it's usually because they have no interest in me as a potential partner.

"You should. I try to be frank with people I trust."

"Okay, so be blunt now. How averse are you to dating on a scale of one to ten?"

"Forty-five." I pause, squinting at the brightness of the sun as a cloud drifts past.

His expression falls. "What if you go with me?"

My heart is staging a coup at the quick change of topic. Is he asking me on a date?

"We could talk to Meg and see if we can double. Maybe getting an outsider's perspective on what I'm doing wrong will help in the long run?"

"Whoa, whoa, you want me to go on a date too?" I say, trying to keep a straight face.

Trey grins. "What? You thought you'd be the third-wheel through all this?"

"Yeah, I was picturing fake mustaches and sunglasses. I'd sit a few tables away and take discrete pictures to discuss after your date. Kind of like film for your games but for dating instead."

Trey lets out one of those deep-belly kind of laughs and I can't help but do the same. Me trying to blend in and spy would be funny and I don't think I'd last more than five minutes.

A few moments pass until we've sobered a bit. He waves to a neighbor who's got to be on the neighborhood gossip chain because she looks like she's taking in every detail of this show.

"What would convince you to do this?" His tone is pleading. I've been learning about the underlying issues people have for their actions, and I'm curious why he's clutching onto this idea so hard.

"Why is it so important that I participate in the dating rituals of the single people? You're kinda my boss now," I say, thinking of this as the strangest work crush I could've come up with. "You have a lot of friends who you've known for lot longer than you've known me. Why not rope them into it?"

He shifts from one foot to the other and stares at me, making me feel like he can see into my brain.

"Because I've never been good at talking about relationships with them. Sports, business, politics, all of which we can have a great discussion. But with relationships, it's almost like we're in competition with each other. And to have someone to talk to and help me out, maybe I'll have a chance at a future with someone." He pauses and says, "And then you'll be over your dating fast and can find happiness with someone too."

The fact he thinks there's a remote chance that a guy would settle for me means he's got a lot to learn. Instead of debating the fact, I muster up all the courage I have.

"What would convince me to do this?" I ask, pausing. And then I have to say it all fast before I run out of guts to get it out. "Is if none of these ladies work out, we'll go on a fun date after."

I think the *fun* part of that demotes the whole meaning I was going for. Do I really want to take a chance on getting my heart broken? To the point that I'll never recover from it? For the guy standing in front of me, I think it's worth a shot.

"Done." Trey grins and reaches out, pulling me into a hug. Every nerve in my body is lighting up like a Christmas tree. I wrap my arms around his middle, for once not trying to pull away like I've touched a live wire.

He lets go and gives me that lopsided grin. How's a girl supposed to resist that?

16

KENZIE

I've taken a lot of chances in my life, but circling back to one that hurt me seems like a bad omen.

After my negotiation discussion with Trey, I called Meg to tell her I'm in for the project. My hands shook the entire time and the only thing that could calm me down was imagining Trey's arms locked around me. It was like five seconds of pure heaven.

Now I'm back at the Love, Austen office after several hours of cleaning up at Dad's. The progress is incredibly slow, but I'd rather do it right and keep my relationship with my dad rather than ruin it with my impatience.

"Kenzie," Meg says, stepping out of her office. "I'm so excited you've decided to take part in this docuseries. From everything Tiffany tells me, you're the one I'm rooting for."

I smile, feeling a little weird that she's hyping me up about dating. Then again this is her business, so maybe that's just a standard part of the process?

"Thank you. I've got an agreement with, um, a friend to do this."

Meg grins and nods. "Okay, well, I've already briefed six of the eight daters. Here's how it's going to go. I'll need you to take the intake test again. I want to make sure we have the most accurate information for your profile."

I nod. "Yeah, I can do that. When are we supposed to start filming?"

I spent last night trying to piece together a contract I can use for my business. It needs another revision and I need a pricing sheet to look semi-professional before I share it with my current and future clients. Trey doesn't seem in a hurry to get his house put together. I mean, the guy hasn't worried about it for the last four weeks like I would've. But I can't avoid the little things forever or my business is going to fall apart before the month is out.

"I'll need to check with the producer of the show, but I think this week," Meg says. "The format will be that we'll get footage of you taking the test, some more of you during your normal life, such as, work, hanging out with friends, etc. Anyone in the video will need to sign a contract that they're okay with their image being used in the films."

"That's understandable."

"Once we've got your intake form done and first interviews filmed, we'll set up each date. There will be four dates total, from men who've matched with you. My guess is they'll start with a match that's in the lower nineties on the scale and then each match will get higher until you are paired up with the guy who is the closest to your match."

I blow out a breath, overwhelmed a bit by the thought of this whole thing.

Meg reaches over and pats my hand in my lap. "I know you've gone through a lot and I want to help avoid any issues you had before. If you don't mind me asking, why did you shut down your account before?"

"I went on fifteen dates with the guys I matched with on the app. The hardest part about that is I had no idea they were ranked on a percentage basis for how well-matched they are. I kept accepting dates from guys because I figured they were a match with me and I might as well give them a chance."

"You didn't see the percent match on your page?" Meg asks, looking worried.

Shaking my head, I said, "No. The fact that users of the app can have a different picture or name on the app does not make things awesome when you go to meet them. Rachelle said you made it that way for the anonymity factor, but the guys I got were all into models and arm candy. I am not that at all. I've got muscles and hips. If I have to put on fifteen pounds of makeup each morning to get a guy to stick around, I'll stay single forever." By the time I'm done with my tirade, my chest is heaving. "Sorry."

Meg waves a hand, pulling me in for a hug. "Don't worry about me. That's something I need to know as the head of the company. Problem solving means we have to get to the root of the problem and then come up with a solution for the mental and emotional wellbeing of our clients. This is real feedback that is valuable for our clients."

I've got tears ready to spill. Meg pulls back and reaches over to grab a tissue from her desk.

"Thanks," I say, blowing my nose.

"Did you have any positive experiences on the app?" Meg's expression is hopeful and I know I'm going to crush that right now.

"I got engaged to someone from the app. But he decided three days later that he didn't want to marry me and moved to another country." I leave out the part about marrying a princess because I don't need to grind Meg's dreams into ash.

She stands. "Let's go take a look, shall we?"

Meg is out of the room in seconds and I hop up to follow her. She's seated behind the large command center and she's already tapping away at the keys on the keyboard.

"What are you doing?" I ask, taking a seat in the chair next to her. It's the same one I sat on for our discussion a few days ago.

"I'm looking up your profile." Meg gives the keyboard another few taps and then points toward the TV screens on the wall.

Kenzie Sullivan, twenty-four.

"I turned twenty-five a few months ago."

Meg nods. "Once the account is shut down, it doesn't update. Reopening it might allow it to update, but I'd rather get more accurate results, especially since you've been through so much."

The screen has several aspects of who I am on the board and it's strange to see it up there as though I'm just a case file.

"Okay, so on that third screen over there is what you should've seen when you started with the app."

There is a list of several profiles with the percentage match of them. None of the names are familiar.

"I've never seen this screen."

Meg does some moving of the mouse to click around on several tabs, pulling up a different screen. "What about this one?"

"That's closer to what I saw, but not exactly. The men's names were there and it would just have a button that said, 'Match Me'."

Meg turns to me, her eyes wide. "That's all it said on there?"

I nod, wondering why that makes a difference.

Again, she clicks several times and opens a new pic that looks exactly like my screen had before.

"Yep, that's it."

Meg glances at me, her eyes sad. "Oh, Kenzie. I'm so, so sorry."

"Are you okay? You look like you're going to tell me I have

cancer or something." I glance around the room, wondering if coming here was a mistake.

"I'm good. I just feel so bad for you. If you were using the app when this photo was up, that means you logged on when we were still in the beta testing version. I had several people test it out for me, making sure they told me everything that worked and what didn't work about the layout. Do you remember how you learned about the app?"

I try to think back and shake my head. "I can't remember."

"No wonder you had such a rough time." She clicks the mouse again and pulls up a new picture. "This is what it should look like in your app today."

The screen is vastly different, showing pictures of actual people and then their match percentage, along with the qualities that match the most.

Glancing up, I try to put into words all that is going on throughout my mind. "So, I'm not the worst loser in the world?"

Meg laughs and her expression turns into a warm smile. "No, I don't think you're a loser at all. Let me show you. What is the name of one of the guys you went on a date with?"

"Johnny Sandoval."

She clicks a few more keys and says, "You two are a twenty-six percent match."

"Yep, that sounds about right."

"Anyone else you want to check?"

"Donovan Gunderson."

There's another pause as she goes to work entering in the information. Pressing the enter key, we both glance up at the screen.

"Thirty-eight percent."

"Will you click on the areas where we did match?" I ask. Johnny wasn't a long-term relationship but Donovan is someone I had spent three days planning to be his future wife.

The screen pops up and it's basically the only two things we both loved. The outdoorsy adventures and the same favorite foods. After turning this info around in my brain, I nod.

"Thank you, Meg. This means a lot."

She pats my hand again and nods. "Well, you're one tough cookie if you had to endure the unpolished version of a match-making app. Thank you for giving me the chance to make it right."

I grin at her, feeling a lift that I hadn't felt since Donovan left.

As I leave the Love, Austen office, I pull out my phone and try to come up with a clever way to tell Trey I'm in.

Maybe I'm not completely cursed when it comes to love. I just had bad luck there for a while.

17

TREY

I can't get Kenzie out of my head. I've thought about sending her a text or two, but I don't want her to think I'm some weirdo who keeps pestering her about doing the matchmaking thing.

The phone rings as I drive back from the Breeze arena, and my mother's name appears on the screen. "Hey, Mom," I say, turning down the road to my home.

"I've got dinner going and I've cooked too much, Trey. Will you come over?"

This doesn't sound suspicious at all. "Mom, if you're inviting someone over to meet me, I'm going to pass."

"I'm serious, Trey. Just come for dinner. It's just your father, sisters and me."

Anything my mom cooks is better than the protein drinks and carrots in my fridge. Then I don't have to eat out either.

"Okay, I'll be there in ten minutes."

Dinner is delicious and as promised, it's just the family. We're in the kitchen doing the dishes, and even though I don't live at home, we still have a rotation for the cleanup. My mother is next to me wiping dry the bigger pots and pans.

"How's the new house, Trey?"

"It's really good. I'm starting to settle in." I use the brush to scrub at the cooked-on sauce from the casserole.

She laughs. "It's about time. I was going to send over a crew of people just to get it all put together."

"Mom, let's be honest. That crew would've been you and the girls."

She gives me a hug around the waist, and I lean into her a bit since my hands are wet from the dishwater.

"I just want to make sure you live a life that you're proud of."

I understand where she's coming from, but I'm also irritated that she can't let me do what I need to do on my timetable. It's her constant hovering and taking over that has made it so I can't even hang up my own television.

"Mom, I am happy. I've achieved something most only dream about. I'm taking steps to find someone to spend my life with, but I need you to cool your jets about it. Let me do this without feeling like there's a deadline I'll never meet."

She takes a step back, her face sobered.

"And as far as the house is coming," I continue, "I hired someone to take it over."

"Really? Who?"

I smile as I think of Kenzie in my home. I'm excited to see what she does with the place, but I'm more curious about whether she'll follow through on the dating docuseries.

"Her name is Kenzie. She's one of Dani's friends. You know, Miles's wife?"

My mother thinks for a moment, wiping at the large serving dish while she thinks. "Did she come to the game when Miles invited me to sit in the box?"

With a nod. "Yes, she was with them."

I have to visibly change my expression when I think of Kenzie's scowl during that first meeting. Mother would latch onto that as the perfect start to a relationship and I'm over here just happy to be friends with the woman who knows a lot about hockey and doesn't use me for the photos.

But does that mean I'm using her for my own comfort in this whole matchmaking contract? I really wish she would send me some kind of answer.

"They were all lovely. Maybe you should take her out on a date."

"We'll see, Mom," I say, handing her the last dish to put in the dishwasher. "I mean, I hired her to do work for me. Isn't that a little weird to be dating someone who will see every embarrassing piece of artwork or macaroni necklace you kept from my childhood?"

She gives me a resigned smile. "Your future wife will see all that anyway." I give her a frown and she says, "All right. If you're working on it, I'll back off."

We finish up and walk out to the family room where my sisters are playing a heated and intense game of Nerts at the card table in the corner. My dad's focus is on the football game on TV.

I take a seat on the couch where my dad has a game on the TV and open my phone. The niggling feeling from a few minutes ago has me wondering if I should've persuaded Kenzie to be part of my madness. There's a whole lot about her background that I haven't learned yet, and probably should've asked before convincing her to take part in the matchmaking event.

Me: I'm sorry I kept bugging you about Love, Austen.

I stare at the screen for several moments as if she'll be available to answer right away.

When the screen goes black, I turn the phone over and focus on the game in front of me. It looks like it's a rerun, but my father's first love is and always will be football, followed closely by hockey.

My phone buzzes and I turn it over, acting as though I'm a teen waiting for his first crush to call him back.

Why did I just think that? Kenzie isn't a crush, although there are a lot of things that could make her fall into that category for me. Then again, she's not into the dating scene and I'm ready to *not* be alone at home. The perfect night would be ordering in takeout, getting comfy in a pair of sweats and a t-shirt, and then cuddling on the couch with my blanket and my girlfriend/fiancée/wife...pending the status of our relationship.

That only brings up the memory of the blanket conversation with Kenzie. I can't help but smile as I think of the bantering.

Kenzie: It's fine. Hillary told me it's time to get back on the ice anyway.

Me: How is dating related to skates?

I see the three dots as I wait for her response.

Kenzie: Because I don't ride horses, so it seemed more appropriate.

I send her a smile emoji.

Me: I'm sorry. Guys can be dumb.

Kenzie: You have no idea.

I laugh, as I can picture her face when she's saying that. A slight frown with her eyebrows raised as if I thought I'd come up with some new theory and she's shooting me down.

Me: Are you coming over tomorrow?

I press send and wish I could take it back. On the one hand, that sentence makes it seem like I'm impatient for her to start and finish organizing my house. On the other, it sounds like we have a completely casual friendship, even though we're still at the beginning stages. It's crazy that I'm comfortable enough for her to just drop by at a moment's notice to hang out. If she wanted, that is.

Nothing comes back for several moments and I'm going through every scenario my last text could've brought up, until she sends another text that reinforces her humor.

Kenzie: Don't we have a date? I mean with other people, of course.

Me: I thought they weren't starting for another week. Wait, did you actually sign up?

Kenzie: Yes, yes I did. If I hate it, I'm blaming you.

Kenzie: Read your emails, Turbo.

That's a new nickname. But I'm stuck on the fact that she's actually going to do this thing with me. I scramble to get into my email app to check her answer. I'll have to move a bunch of stuff around if she's right.

The email isn't hard to spot and I groan as I read that we're supposed to meet for the preliminary interviews tomorrow morning at the Love, Austen office.

Me: Point goes to Kenzie for paying attention in class.

Kenzie: (sends me an emoji of a blonde woman saying, "What? Like it's Hard?")

Me: Who is that? And I just saw that we're starting on Wednesday. So, we'll have two more days until Date #1.

Kenzie: Let me guess. You've never watched a romantic comedy in your life.

Me: Buzzer sound. Errrr! Wrong. I have three sisters. I'm fluent in *How to Lose a Guy in 10 Days*.

Kenzie: Interesting.

Me: That's all I get? Interesting?

Me: You must like chick flicks. Who is the woman in the meme? And what other random tidbit of information are you willing to share?

Seconds tick by and my dad is trying to get me into the football game. I'm almost tempted to look up the final score and stats of the game so I can zone out.

Kenzie: So many questions. It's Elle Woods from *Legally Blonde*. And random is my middle name, so you might need to be more specific.

Me: Where's your favorite place to eat in Boston?

Kenzie: At the moment, my house because it's cheap or free. But when I get a paycheck, anywhere that serves steak.

"What are you grinning at?" My dad asks, causing me to jump. "You're over here laughing and the quarterback for the Patriots has been sacked twice."

"I'm not laughing at the TV, Dad," I say. Standing, I stretch, still smiling at the random conversation we've had over text.

I walk into the kitchen and grab a cup, filling it up from the faucet and take a long swig.

Me: Well, I owe you something now that you're going to join the dating chaos. What do you want?

The three dots start and stop so many times that I've lost count.

Kenzie: If you like what I do when I organize your house, tell people. A growing business will help me forget the fact that I'm actually dating.

I sit there and marvel. It's rare for people to pass up money or expensive gifts, especially from a professional athlete like me. That just adds to the positive column for Kenzie.

Me: Okay, but what else? There's got to be something I can do.

I finish my drink and put it in the dishwasher. My mother comes into the kitchen and says, "Are you leaving already?"

With a nod, I say, "Yeah, I've got a long day tomorrow."

"Take this box of leftovers. You know your sisters won't eat them and I'd hate for them to go bad."

I lean over and give her a kiss on the cheek. "Thanks, Mom. Okay, tell the family bye for me."

My mom waits at the door as I walk down to my car. "Let me know if your dating plans change. I've got a list of young women you'd be perfect for."

Shaking my head, I get into the car and breathe. It's hard for a mother to see past the bias of her child, especially in seeing compatible traits in the opposite sex.

Kenzie: We've already agreed that if it doesn't work out with the others, we'll go on a fun date. That's enough...

Me: Dates are usually fun.

Kenzie: Not in my experience.

Me: Then both sides have been doing it wrong. I'll plan on it.

As I drive home, I wonder what a "fun" date would consist of for Kenzie. I'd need a lot more to go on if I'm going to be breaking any of her preconceived notions.

But we'll have to get through the dates we're matched with first.

18

KENZIE

Working for Trey is already hard and I'm only on day two. Well, technically day one, since the last time consisted of a twenty-minute tour.

The guy looks so dang good every time he appears, whether it's with a sweaty t-shirt or a good-looking polo shirt. And here I am in my joggers and t-shirt, hoping to make some good progress on this job without ruining any of my good clothes. The sooner I finish, the faster I can move on without getting attached.

The start date for Trey's house wasn't supposed to be until later in the week, but the dumpster at my dad's won't be emptied until tomorrow and my brother's truck is in the shop. I'd rather not move the bags a second time, even if I get an arm workout in. A huge part of the hoard cleaning is mental gymnastics and I figured I could see a bigger difference today while working at Trey's.

It doesn't hurt that our texting session from the day before made me laugh several times. So that could be part of the reason I'm here.

I start with cleaning out all the cabinets in the kitchen. I'm not the tallest girl in the world and have to use one of the bar stools to see the top shelves. Once that's done, I pull over the few boxes against the wall near the kitchen table.

The first is full of clothing. Wrong place to be storing these, Trey.

The next one has a few plates and several plastic cups. I place those on the bottom shelf of the cupboard next to the sink. The plates go on the lowest shelf by the stove. The most logical places to need the dinnerware in a pinch.

The two forks in his one drawer are part of a four-piece set I find in a smaller box, along with a few canned goods.

"How long has he lived here?" I say out loud when I've put all the boxes away. It looks more like Mother Hubbard lives here than a professional athlete.

"Four and a half weeks," a voice says, and I whirl around to see Trey grinning at me from the doorway. At least he's fully clothed right now. "You don't like my selection of food?"

I open the fridge and see only protein drinks and a small bag of carrots. "I'm thinking you're either not much of a cook or you're Bugs Bunny."

He laughs and says, "I do like my carrots. I credit them with not needing glasses. Cooking isn't my forte and I'm not home that often yet. The off-season means I can actually hang out with my friends when I want and this is one of those days when I'll pick up something to eat while I'm out with the guys."

I nod, shutting the door. "You're not into the clean-eating thing I've heard most hockey players do?"

"I usually do, but I get my food from a chef." His expression is pained, almost like he's embarrassed to say that.

With a shrug, I say, "You might as well. I mean, food is the fuel to help your performance, right?"

"Are you into cooking?"

I laugh, thinking of my lack of abilities in the kitchen. "I do a lot of meal prep with things that are already cooked. Less chance of a fire that way."

He laughs, the sound coming from deep down and I have to look away so I don't focus on the beautiful outline of his jaw, the bright white of his teeth. Yep, I need to get this job done as soon as possible before I start obsessing.

"Well, we're going to have to get some more things to fill the shelves in here. Maybe some more place settings so you can have your friends over every once in a while?"

"That sounds like a great idea. When you've got an idea for other stuff to buy, we'll go shopping."

His words make me gulp. I can barely function with him during the limited stints at his house, let alone spend hours going through stores to buy things for his home.

"Let's take this one step at a time, Turbo," I say, trying to walk past him. I've never been this close. Okay, that's a lie. The last time I was this close to him, aside from the hug he gave me on his front sidewalk yesterday, he was probably seventy pounds lighter and six inches shorter, but he smells so good right now that I almost go blank on being the strong, independent type.

"Turbo, huh? Why do you say that?"

Finally, something to clear my mind. Hockey can always do that. "You do a great job of pumping your team up, of doing everything you can to keep them motivated. But most of the time you use up so much energy hyping that you don't have as much for game time."

"Good to know that my nickname comes from a place of love," he says with a grin.

That four-letter word shouldn't be said within my vicinity. Ever. Not from those lips.

"I'm just here to get your life organized."

I hope he stays where he is but once I step into his room, I can see he's right behind me.

He clears his throat and says, "It sounds like you know quite a bit about hockey. I take it you're an avid fan?"

"The ice is home for me. I didn't realize that until I'd been gone from it for a while." Lame Donovan.

He sits on the corner of his bed as I drag a few boxes away from the wall just three feet from him.

"I need to hear the story."

"Why?" I ask, turning to him with a frown.

"Because my curiosity is like a cat and I'll be coming up with scenarios for the rest of the day." We sit there staring at one another for several seconds, a charge of tension thick between us.

Instead of answering, I turn back to the box, pulling out several long-sleeved shirts.

Trey asks, "Okay, how about we do an exchange? I'll tell you a rough dating story and you tell me one of yours?"

I scoff, knowing mine is hard to top, even if he's a celebrity.

"I'm listening," I say, still focused on the clothes. There's a lot to do and I still need to get as much done here before we have to film. Every spare moment will be split between organizing Trey's house and my dad's. I had nightmares last night that I got lost forever in my dad's hoard. Hopefully my work doesn't constantly take over sleep as my business grows.

"My mother thinks I should've been married three years ago," Trey begins.

"Are you kidding? You'd just gotten into the NHL and–" I clamp my mouth shut. I'm just an excited fan who's had a crush on the guy since I was a teenager.

Trey smiles and I focus on folding the shirts to fit into the drawers. If I can't see his grin, maybe I'll keep this as close to a client relationship as possible.

"Exactly. There was a lot going on at the time. I was lucky to have gotten drafted to my hometown team and that I moved up to the pros as soon as I did. Those two years with the farm team were tough."

"Okay, so you have a loving mother who is probably hoping to have grandbabies. Have you tried listening to her?" Where is this coming from? Why am I encouraging him to find the latest shiny object and go for a relationship?

Because guys who don't get intimidated by women who play sports and play them well are unicorns. I was the girl who could drop by at any hour and play Fortnite or Super Smash Bros. in sweats and be treated like one of the guys at college. I wasn't the kind of girl a guy has on his arm at fancy events. And then the end of my relationship with Donovan sealed the deal. I'm a perma-friend.

"Have I tried dating? Yes, yes I have." His tone is irritated and I have to hide the smile that I caused that.

"Well, what's the problem then? Do you have an incurable medical disease? I can see it now: you'll be in diapers in ten years and the ladies aren't going for it."

The room is silent for several moments and then Trey bursts out laughing, to the point that he falls back on the bed.

"You're funny, Kenzie. Unexpectedly funny."

I feign a frown and say, "What? Why is that surprising?"

He sits up and I catch a glimpse of the muscles as his t-shirt inches its way back down. "Well, every time I've met you, you're a little closed off. I just mean, it's nice to see another side of you. The side that isn't so serious."

I stiffen with that comment. That cannot happen. There can be no softening of feelings between us. Different worlds, Kenzie.

"I don't know about you, but I have this boss who is so ornery, he wants me to get things put together as soon as possible."

Trey shakes his head. "I never said that."

"How do you know I'm talking about you?" I say, opening another box.

"Because I know you're working at your dad's. I figured you would be teasing about me."

"Okay," I admit. "I might've been joking a bit, but I really need to get this part of your house crossed off my list for today."

He stands up and raises his hands in surrender. "I'll get out of your hair. I actually have to run some errands. But I left my phone number and a key to the house on the kitchen table for you. That way you don't have to wait for me to get the door every time, or if you need to work while I'm gone."

The way he says it deflates all the excitement I've had while flirting with him the past few minutes. "Sounds good. Thanks."

I pull out my earbuds and connect them to an audiobook that isn't drawing my attention.

Not a whole lot can compete with Trey Hatch.

19

TREY

I'm packed in a room with six other daters. Three women and three men plus me. Where is Kenzie? I've got a chair right next to the door and I keep glancing up, wondering what is taking her so long. Hopefully she didn't change her mind in the six hours since we last texted. She said she'd be here and the woman is usually early.

"Welcome to all," Meg says, glancing around the room. "We're so happy to have you here. There's so much that goes into the matching process and we hope that through this docuseries, more people will be comfortable with the idea. I hope all of you find at least one of your matches to be the person you want to start a relationship with."

She pauses and the group claps. I'm trying to smile and listen, but it's hard when I'm waiting for the woman who makes me laugh at her dry humor and cracks jokes about my hockey skills.

I found my polo shirt today because she'd hung it up from one of the boxes I'd left in the kitchen.

"Okay, we are going to start with your intake tests. It will be a list of multiple-choice answers that help us understand more about you and your priorities when it comes to the people we match you with. There will also be a written section for you to fill out that will give us a more in-depth look at how to zone in on the right matches. We only have three computers working now, so we'll have to take turns. You three first," she says, pointing to the ones closest to her.

The door opens and shuts, revealing Kenzie. She glances up and sees Meg. "Sorry I'm late." There's no other explanation or excuse.

She sees me and sits down in the chair next to me. "Hey," she says, dropping a large over-the-shoulder bag on the ground.

"Who's late now?"

She rolls her eyes. "Yeah, yeah. I didn't set an alarm and got in a groove cleaning up my dad's place. I barely had enough time to shower and make it here."

"You're shaking."

Kenzie takes in a deep breath. "Casualty of being an ex-athlete. Being late usually meant–"

"Punishment," we both say together.

"What was your least favorite punishment?"

She lets out a deep laugh. "Lines. I still have nightmares about the red line every once in a while."

"You played hockey?"

Another laugh and a nod. "Why do you think I like hockey so much? I played in college."

I can't believe I didn't pick up that information sooner. "I should've known that."

"Well, you're still playing and you earn money from it. Some of us mere mortals have to resort to the rec league and do other things to live." She leans over and gives me a quick nudge with her elbow, probably the first time she's initiated contact with me since we've hung out/interviewed for her position.

"I can only imagine how hard it is. I heard you work for a guy who stores his clothes in boxes in the kitchen."

She feigns exasperation but then bursts out laughing once she looks back at me. "I still can't believe you did that. Did you ever change the load of clothes to the dryer?"

I give her a frown. "Maybe. I threw a bunch of clothes in together and didn't see my red shirt in the pile. I only have pink socks now." I lift up my pant leg to show her.

"That is the best thing I've seen today. Too bad you're not wearing shorts so you could show those bad boys off."

I nod, trying to keep a straight face but crack when I say, "I'll take that under advisement."

Her phone rings and she glances around surveying the room before she picks it up and walks out the door. "Hey Mom," is all I hear before the door closes.

She's mentioned her father a lot, but I haven't heard anything about her mom. Instead, I get a text from my own.

Mom: I saw Sandra Taylor at the store. Her daughter is still waiting for you to give her a call back after your date a few months ago.

Me: Mom, I told you to let me be. If I wanted to go out with what's-her-face, I would've called already.

Mom: Gotcha. Well, I'm going to the store later. Do you need me to pick up some food?

And now I'm embarrassed. I've been working so hard to figure things out on my own and act grown up. As easy as it would be to have my mom go grocery shopping for me, there are some things I need to learn as an adult man with an over-protective mother.

Me: I'm planning to go on the way home.

Mom: Where are you now?

I let the screen turn black and put the phone back into my pocket. Answering Mom is going to have to wait until I can come up with a concise statement as to what I'm doing.

It's been a while and the first group of daters hasn't finished in the computer room. We're going to be here forever.

Kenzie comes back when the second group rotates in to take their test. "What did I miss?"

"Not a whole lot yet," I say, still irritated that my mom is prying into my love life even after I asked her not to.

Meg waves us over and shows us several spots where we have to sign. Kenzie takes a pen and starts scribbling her signature across the pages like she's used to signing autographs for people. I'm wondering if I need to wait and have Miles or Dave look at the contract.

"I already sent them to your agent, Trey," Meg says, with a grin. "He made a few marks on what needed to change, so we'll be good to go." She points out a couple minor differences from the regular contract and I breathe a sigh of relief.

"Who knew there was this much paperwork to sign?" Kenzie says, rubbing around her wrist.

"That's why I'm all for the digital signing. Then I don't have to have the paper copy sitting around."

Kenzie shakes her head. "You've got plenty of paper at your house already. I can't imagine more paperwork with all the endorsement deals you have going on."

"Exactly."

It's finally our turn in the computer room. Kenzie takes a seat at the computer to the right and I have to sit with my back to her, since the computer next to her is turned off.

"Here we go," I say, following the very strict instructions on the paper next to me.

The click of the mouse behind me causes me to turn. "You're already answering questions? How are you that fast?"

"I already had an account, remember? I just had to login." She goes back to answering the questions and I'm still waiting for the blue circle of death to finish loading whatever the next page will be.

A sheet of paper sits against the wall and I grab it, tearing off a small piece and rolling it between my fingers. I flick it backwards, but get no reply. A few more with bigger sections of paper and they start flying back at me.

"Keep your paper to yourself," Kenzie says with a laugh. "Some of us have to get back to work after this."

"Should we race to see who gets done first?" I ask, dreading the fact that there are one hundred and twenty-five questions.

"I think I'm going to win. You just ripped up your portion of the written exam."

Turning the paper over, I see the questions with several lines below each one for the written answer.

"Okay, well, don't leave without me."

"We still have the first interviews today. I think we'll both be here for a while. There's one woman who looks like she's a talker. I can only imagine how much editing they'll have to do," Kenzie says.

"Psst," I say, trying to contain my laughter. "What did you put for question number one?"

"Trey Hatch," Kenzie says, turning around. "Do I need to send you to the principal's office?" She manages to have a stone-cold expression until the very end.

I nod a few times and say, "Yeah, this does feel like I'm back in school again but don't know any of the answers to the test."

Kenzie laughs and says, "Trey, this is supposed to be a personal test about your likes and dislikes. You better answer it honestly or you might end up with me."

"What's wrong with that?" I ask, staring into her eyes when she turns around in shock.

We sit there for several long moments and a knock on the door causes us to break the staring contest.

"How's it going in here?" Meg asks, glancing between the two of us.

"I'm going to need a new paper," I say, holding up the ripped one.

Meg chuckles and says, "I can do that. We're almost ready for the next first interview, so let me know when you've finished." She shuts the door and I go back to staring at the screen, wondering what she meant.

I can't concentrate on the questions on the screen, only wondering why Kenzie would make it sound like the worst thing to be matched to her. The woman can make anything funny and has a lot of depth I didn't see before.

"I'm done," Kenzie says a few minutes later.

A glance at the screen tells me I'm only on question twenty-five. "Okay, well, good luck on camera."

She gives me a smile and then walks out of the room. Something about the last few minutes was like a switch to the atmosphere in the room.

It takes every brain cell in me to finish out the test, all the while wondering what Kenzie put for her answers. What would happen if we were matched? A shot of excitement shoots through me. I can see a future with Kenzie. That might be a bit premature given the fact I haven't finished this test, but I'm suddenly hoping she's on my list of potential dates.

20

KENZIE

I'm still kicking myself for turning the attention to the remote possibility that Trey would be matched to me. It's possible he didn't even register the words, but I hurry through the test to get out of the room because I'm starting to overheat.

Now I'm sitting in a chair that is cutting off the circulation to my thighs. It's up high enough that my legs dangle. Bright lights shine behind me and to the side, in front and what seems like all over. Do interviews have to feel like you're baking on the surface of the sun?

A woman who looks familiar has someone fixing her makeup and I remember that Evie's strict instruction was to apply lip gloss before the cameras start rolling. I dig the tube out of my pocket and apply, watching as the makeup artist applies lipstick to the woman's lips.

My lips are starting to tingle, but I push that aside. I've got to get through this interview, which right now seems worse than the time I had to play through a broken wrist against our school's rival.

"Hi, I'm Samantha Jordan, host of the Everything Your

Heart Desires show. I've got several questions to ask here. Answer them as thoroughly as you'd like. Just remember that single word answers will not be accepted."

Why do I feel like I'm on a game show right now?

"Okay," I mumble, trying to get comfortable in the chair. And I've already broken that one rule. I don't care right now though because my lips feel like I've just eaten a jalapeno pepper, seeds and all. I barely tolerate spice so I'm trying to make sure everything is okay, at least from the camera's point of view.

"Tell us about yourself, Kenzie," Samantha says.

"I'm Kenzie Sullivan, twenty-five from Boston."

The woman nods. "What are some of your favorite things to do?"

I try to smile, the urge to itch just below my lip line is getting to me now. "I love to play hockey and I am a professional organizer."

"That's interesting. How did you get into that?"

The heat in my lips makes it so I can't fully focus on what she's asking. "Um, I, uh, have learned a lot about cleaning, working on my dad's home growing up. Sorry, can I get a glass of water?" I ask, turning around to some of the crew.

It takes a few seconds for them to bring a bottle of water and I take a few long swallows, then pucker my lips so I can let some of the cool water wash over them from the bottle. It only lessens the pain though.

"Okay, let's continue," Samantha says, giving me a glare like I just forgot her birthday. "Why did you want to come on this show?"

I'm sweating right now and can't think clearly to answer. I blink several times, before raising the bottle to my lips again.

"We need to answer the question," Samantha says again.

"I made her," Trey says from the wings. I turn to see him

smiling as he strides toward me. He turns enough that the camera doesn't see his mouth, "Are you okay?"

I pull the bottle away from my lips and his reaction of terror has me wondering what I look like. Instead of worrying about the cameras, I pull out my phone and turn on the selfie camera.

Letting out a shriek, I clap my hand over my mouth. My lips are bright red and at least three times bigger than normal. Small bubbles have formed around the edges.

"I look like Botox gone wrong," I say.

"Cut," Samantha says. "What happened?"

Trey's eyes are on me, worry written all over his face. "Are you allergic to something you ate?"

I shook my head. "I haven't eaten since we got here."

"You did apply lip gloss," Samantha says. "I've heard that people can be allergic to certain types. Have you used it before?"

"No," I say, pulling out the tube again. "My roommate told me to try it."

"You might want to go out and get something to help calm the swelling. We'll just have to do your first interview another time." She glances down at the paper on her lap. "Trey?"

"That's me."

"You're up last."

"I think I'll wait and do my interview when Kenzie does hers." Trey puts a hand on my shoulder and I give him a small, painfilled smile.

Samantha stands from her chair. "We need to get this done so the editors can cut them all together for the first episode."

"Well, they'll have to wait on mine then too. We need to get Kenzie some help." He reaches over and takes my hand in his, gently tugging me up out of the chair. We leave the room and even though the skin on my lips is stretched tight from being swollen, I'm grinning. This pain is worth it.

Once outside the office, Trey turns and says, "What should we do?"

"About this?" I ask, pointing to my lips. "I'm not sure. What do you think?"

He shrugs. "I'm not really good at the first aid kind of stuff. My mom just knew what to do and I always followed her instructions." His eyes go wide. "Maybe I'll call her?"

I nod. "Go for it. My mother is more into brand name clothes rather than knowing the brands of medicines."

We walk, still hand in hand, down the sidewalk. I catch a glimpse of me in one of the windows. "I look like Will Smith in *Hitch.*"

"Huh?" Trey asks, trying to understand what I mean.

"You really need a chick flick education, Trey," I say, doing my best to laugh without using my lips.

Trey puts the phone away. "Are you okay if we go to my parents' house? It's not too far from here and we can get you something. You look like you're in pain."

"Well, my lips have swelled up like balloons and I'm pretty sure the blisters are only going to get worse."

He squeezes my hand and leads me to a public parking garage. "We'll take my car."

"Why are you doing this?" I ask, curious. None of my former boyfriends would've done much except tell me to see a doctor.

"I don't want to see you in pain." He opens the door for me, making sure I get in okay before shutting it.

It's strange to be on this side of his car, since the last time I was in it I was driving him home after he got hit on the head.

He's right about his parents living close to the office. He guides me inside with his hand on the small of my back and I have to focus on the stinging pain of my lips instead of letting my imagination run wild.

"Mom, we're here."

I recognize her from the box suite at the Breeze game a couple weeks ago. "It's nice to see you again," I say, but the words don't sound quite right coming out.

"Oh, you poor dear. Come in here and we'll get you all fixed up." She takes me by the arm and leads me into a bathroom. It looks like Trey warned her because she's got out a box of first aid supplies and a damp cloth. "Take this and wipe gently on your lips. That will hopefully take off whatever is causing the swelling."

I wince at first from the pain, but the cooling sensation of the cloth helps to battle against the raging fire of my lips.

"Do you know what caused it?" Mama Hatch asks.

"Lip gloss," Trey says, leaning against the doorframe.

She gives him a disbelieving look and turns back to me. "What were you doing?"

"An interview for a dating thing," I say. My cheeks have now taken on the flames and I'm just going to go hide in a cave for the rest of my life.

Mama Hatch turns to Trey. "What kind of dating thing?"

Trey doesn't look like he wants to respond to that. "It's something Dave set me up with. Kenzie and I will be on a matchmaking docuseries where we'll go on dates with people we've matched with."

She turns back to me, her eyebrow raised. "Is that true?"

I nod. "Yes."

"You don't believe me, Mom?" Trey says, pretending to be offended.

"Well, you had the chance to tell me earlier but you didn't. So your agent set you up for this, Trey," she says, then turning to look back at me, "but why are you part of it? You're such a darling girl, I wouldn't think you'd need help in the dating department."

"I'm just getting burned left and right over here," Trey mumbles.

Laughing is like a reflex here. "Yeah, uh, I'm a cat lady in the making."

"Oh, Kenzie, I thought that once, too. But sometimes, we just go on dates with all the wrong people. If this matchmaking thing doesn't work out, I'll take care of you."

It's hard to keep a straight face with Trey in the background making faces and mouthing the word, "No."

Mama Hatch purses her lips and turns around. "This is why you wanted me to back off on setting you up?" There is a touch of bitterness to her words.

"Mom, I'm grateful that you care about me the way you do. It's just hard when you think I'll magically have a long-term relationship with Betty-down-the-street's cousin twice removed when you haven't even met her."

Now I feel like I'm intruding on a private moment. Mama Hatch nods, pinching her lips between her teeth. She rummages through a box and pulls out a few pink gel caps. "Benadryl. This should help the swelling to go down. Let's go get you a drink of water to wash those down."

She takes a step around Trey, and I glance up at him. There's sadness there. On impulse, I lean in and give him a quick hug. In a surprising twist, he pulls me in and the comfort is next level.

I don't want to tug away, but finally do enough to look up at him again. "I should probably go get those pills. Otherwise, I'll be sailing the skies from the size of my lips."

He lets out a low laugh, nodding. I step around him and walk toward the noise from the kitchen.

"Does he really think all that?" Mama Hatch asks me once she hands me the glass of water.

"We've never talked much about past dates," I say, truthfully. I take in a big swallow of water and take the pills. Once they're down, I hand her back the glass.

"Here's a tube of some lip ointment. Hopefully it will help

ease the pain of the blisters. You poor girl." She takes my hand in hers and pats it a few times, a slow smile appears. "And what's your relationship to my Trey?"

"Um, we are, um, he's kind of my boss. I'm organizing his house."

She blinks a few times and says, "That's right. I'm excited to see what you do with the place. It's got such great character, but the boxes everywhere take away from it."

"The boxes that are in the wrong place altogether."

Mama Hatch grins and says, "You just might be perfect for him. I'll keep my fingers crossed you somehow manage to get matched."

Shaking my head, I say, "I doubt that will happen."

"You don't want it to?" she asks, her eyes boring into me.

What a complex question.

I glance behind me, making sure Trey isn't within earshot. Leaning in, I whisper, "I'd be okay with dating him." I press my pointer finger to my lips to signal she needs to stay quiet, but wince at the pain there.

"Put that ointment on and I hope to see you again soon, Kenzie." She winks and then opens the dishwasher and starts to unload them.

I smile and nod, wincing again at the soft burn still coursing through my lips. Opening the tube she gave me, I smell it first, wondering if it will be worse than the lip gloss. What if the swelling spreads to the rest of my face?

I might as well risk it for the comfort. I spread a thin layer of the ointment on my lips. Several seconds pass and the pain doesn't rise. Maybe I'm safe.

"Thanks, Mom," Trey says, leaning over to give her a kiss on the cheek.

"I've got a few things to send with you. Do you like zucchini, Kenzie?" she asks me.

I've only had it a few times plain, but I've always enjoyed the zucchini bread my grandma used to make. "Sure."

"Oh good. My garden is overproducing this year and I'm just looking for people who need vegetables."

"That makes it nice, so you don't have to go to the store as often," I say, not sure how to respond. How does one have a conversation about zucchini? Is it some adult level merit badge I haven't unlocked yet?

She turns and walks into what looks like a pantry and comes out with two large bags of zucchini, peppers, and lettuce from what I can see.

"I'll give these to Kenzie, since I know Trey will let them rot in his fridge," she says with a wink. "Trey, I've got a few boxes of leftovers you can have for meals when you need."

The bag is identical to the one she gave me, except it's stacked with black boxes of food. "Is she your chef?" I ask, curious. He said he usually only ate food from a chef.

He grins and nods. "My mom is great at making the healthy stuff and she insisted on continuing that when I made it onto the Breeze."

I smile. My mother is an amazing woman. Not the most nurturing, but she's always been happy for me when I achieve the goals I've set out for myself. But Mama Hatch is on a whole new level. Maybe a tad bit overkill, but it seems she's got a heart of gold.

We say goodbye and I walk to the car, grateful I won't have to take the train anywhere with my lips sticking out like a duck. I can only imagine the looks I'd get.

"Where to?" Trey asks.

"Home. I'm going to need a nap after the embarrassment of today."

He shakes his head. "It could happen to anyone."

He drives me to the Spice House and makes sure I get to the front door. "Is anyone else here?"

"No, they're all at work."

"What happens if you pass out or something?" he asks, and I can tell he's picturing it now.

With a laugh, I say, "Trey, I'm not going to pass out from a lip allergy. I'll be fine."

"Are you sure? I could stay for a bit. Make sure you get everything you need."

"You want to stay? Don't you have training to get to?" I ask, trying to keep my emotions in check.

He nods. "I'll get to it later."

"Trey, the lip gloss isn't your fault," I say, trying to figure out the real reason he's wanting to hang out longer.

"I know, but maybe you wouldn't be in this mess if I didn't bug you to join the docuseries."

I turn to him, putting a hand on his upper arm. "Trey, I decided to give this a try for several reasons. If you keep blaming yourself for every little thing that happens, that's like not trusting me to make a decision on my own."

It takes a few seconds for that to sink in. "I'm sorry, I didn't think of it that way. I thought I guilted you into doing it."

"No guilt here. I might as well try something new when I have the chance to." I pause for a moment and then say, "If you want to stay, we can start you on your knowledge of some of the best movies out there."

"Chick flicks?" he says with a half-smile that sends my stomach for a flip.

"Yep. Then you'll always have something to talk about when you're on a date with women."

Not that I want to ponder that statement too much. The jealousy dragon inside me will awaken and take over.

21

TREY

"**D**o you need another pillow?" I ask, eyeing the one on the opposite couch. As of right now, I've got Kenzie propped up on at least four pillows and tucked a blanket around her.

She reaches out and holds me down when I try to stand. "Trey, I'm fine. You're treating me like I'm fragile. I've taken a lot of hits before, breaking several bones. This is just a small thing." She points to her lips, which look like they've gone down at least a little.

"I just want to help," I say, sighing.

"I know, and I appreciate that. But let's settle in and watch the movie. Is this what your mom did every time you got sick?"

Her words prompt a surge of memories of sick days growing up. "Yep. She'd make homemade chicken noodle soup and let me sleep on the couch most of the day."

"Wow, that sounds amazing. Ramen noodles were the only option in the Sullivan household."

She starts the movie and I turn over our conversation in my mind. There are a lot of things I didn't realize when it came to the opposite sex. I've never compared childhood sick days with my guy friends and I'm beginning to see just how much my mother went above and beyond to take care of me and my sisters.

"Why were you so bugged with your mom earlier?" Kenzie asks.

I shake my head, not happy with my small outburst this afternoon. "I shouldn't have been so stern about it. It's hard when she doesn't listen to what I actually want. The other night I told her I hired you and she said that she was happy she didn't have to come over with my sisters to unpack me. The hardest part is I'm a grown man, and there are some basic skills I don't have because of her love to help. I guess I just want her to trust me that I'll find someone who will be a good fit for me."

"Understandable," Kenzie says. She turns to watch the show she'd mentioned at the interview. Will Smith is on a double date and ends up having an allergic reaction to the fish.

"This is what you were talking about," I say, grinning.

"You're learning, Boss," she says, chuckling.

"Boss, huh? I kind of like the sound of that."

She shakes her head. "Don't get too used to it. I'll be at your house for two weeks and then you'll be rid of me."

Something about her words hits me in the gut and I try to imagine a future without Kenzie in any capacity.

"I don't think so. I'm pretty sure you're stuck with me."

"What if you get a girlfriend? Women get very jealous of 'the friend' when they're in a relationship."

"Emphasis on 'if' there. Most women get jealous that I'm married to my career."

Kenzie lets out a long sigh. "Then you're with the wrong woman. She should be cheering you on and helping you stay consistent in your game rather than worrying about how much time you spend with her."

I study her profile, trying to figure her out. "You wouldn't get bugged when your partner tells you he has to go last minute, several times a week?"

"If it happens daily for several months, sure. But there's only so much time you'll get to play hockey. You can both make it work."

"How?" I'm extra curious because I've never had a good solution to this dilemma. Putting in a hundred and ten percent is standard for me. I'm guessing that's why nothing has worked out in the love sector before. If Kenzie has the golden key to opening that vault of wisdom, I'm all ears.

"She can travel with you to away games. There are opportunities to work with the hockey organizations too. And then when you do have time, you make sure to spend all that time with her, rather than your attention divided."

"If only it were that easy." I pause and decide to ask the question siren in my brain. "If you were to marry a hockey player, what would you do?"

She smiles at me. "I have the advantage of skating. So, if he needs to go blow off steam over his last game, I'd go with. I'd try to travel to as many games as possible with him and then make sure to hold up life once we had kids and stuff. You can make a takeout dinner in a hotel room just as romantic as dinner at a five-course restaurant. I think it's a lot about balance and talking. I'm not always good at the communication part of life, but it's important."

I nod. The fact that Kenzie talks about life as a hockey wife with such ease makes me wonder if she's real. Most of the women I've dated have been more worried about going out to fancy dinners and what the latest expensive trend is in the clothing and accessory part of life.

More wisdom from the Book of Kenzie. If she wasn't in pain, I'd be tempted to kiss her right here.

22

KENZIE

"Breathe," Hillary says. Evie is to my right, rubbing my back for comfort as I breathe into a paper bag. Who knew that really worked?

It's been three days since the burning lips incident and I almost look like myself. My time with Trey is like a golden memory in my brain. Him fawning all over me and our conversations mean that much more.

His questions about what life as a hockey wife would look like make me want that even more. Too bad we're stuck under contract for four dates.

But now I'm back to reality. Date #1 is today.

"You're going to be just fine, Kenz," Evie says. I can see her smile from my peripheral vision.

I pause and say, "Will I though? I think I need a few more days to process this."

"A few more days is only going to mean that you'll try to delay it again," Hillary says. "Donovan was a tool to leave you the way he did. That doesn't mean you can't find your happiness now."

I frown, dropping my head to rest on my crossed arms on the table.

"My happily ever after would be with the guy who convinced me to go along with this in the first place." I think of Trey's sweet texts making sure I was okay even after he left the other night.

"Did you say that to him?" Evie asks, and she's so close that I end up jumping.

"She told him that if he didn't find someone to date after this, they'd go on a *'fun'* date," Hillary says, putting too much emphasis on the fun part.

"Oh!" Evie says, looking a little concerned. "What are we trying to say with a fun date? Aren't they all supposed to be fun?"

"Not in my experience. Besides, I figured it would be a more casual thing, since all of these dates will be recorded." I stand up and walk over to my bookshelf. There's half of a large Hershey's hidden next to the book I'd shown my roommates. I need some chocolate running in my veins if I'm going to survive today.

"Are you secretly hoping he'll figure out that you're his soulmate and that it will all work out?"

I shake my head. "If my luck ran that direction, sure. But at this point, I just need to get my business off the ground and survive the next couple weeks." But there had been hand holding and protecting. Babying even to make sure I was comfortable. And his mother's face when I admitted I want to date Trey.

I wave that off. He could be that affectionate helping an old woman across the street for all I know. It doesn't highlight that I'm anything special.

"How many dates do you have to go on in that time? And how do they pick?" Evie asks.

"When I talked to Meg last, she said it would be four dates over the next two weeks. They'll wait to release the videos weekly, so we'll have to keep things quiet for a bit."

Four dates. Not only would I have to watch some other girl with her hands all over Trey, I'd have to endure the torture myself. Strike that. There won't be hands on me because I'll pull out my pretend ninja skills and have at him if my date touches me inappropriately. Dating is torture in general.

"What time is your date?" Hillary asks, leaning on the table so we're eye to eye when I finally look up. She's holding a mascara wand, waving it around as she speaks and I lean back. I've already had duck lips this week. I don't need to start investing in eye patches.

I check the time on my phone. "In about an hour."

"What's the activity? We need to get you ready, girl." I hold still as Hillary starts painting my eyelashes with the wand.

This morning I'd woken up to a few details about Date #1 but I hadn't finished reading the text before I started googling how to fake sick so people believe you. I open the text again and groan. "We're going for a swan boat ride on the Charles and then to dinner. Todd likes gaming and cooking."

"That will be fun. Plenty of time to get to know your date. You haven't dated him before, right?" Hillary says, tossing the mascara tube back into her makeup bag. She picks up a tub of creamy beige and I shake my head.

"Mascara is enough for today. I don't need to puff up like a blueberry because I'm allergic to your makeup." I close my eyes and picture that scene. "No, I haven't dated this guy before. Since they activated my dormant profile, I've been matched with some new people, which I hope works out."

"Did you look him up on the app?" Evie asks. "I thought the app was supposed to nominate the top three who will match closest to you. You should be able to see them, right?"

I shrug. "Meg says their profiles will be blocked to give us a more authentic reaction when we meet them. Let's be honest, girls. I don't think life will be any different after this is over."

In an act that I would've suspected Hillary to do instead, Evie grabs me by the shoulders and gives me a good shake. "Come on, Kenzie. You are amazing. Just because you've been around some deadbeats doesn't mean you shouldn't have your own happily ever after. Sure, we can do it on our own, but it's kind of nice to have a built-in best friend. Until they leave of course."

Hillary and I train our gaze on Evie. "Did you have a relationship like that?" I ask.

"Yes. Give me the tea," Hillary says.

Evie glances down at her hands before looking back up. "I was married for two weeks."

My jaw drops open. Surprised is an understatement.

"Evie, I can't imagine divorcing someone. What happened?" I ask.

"We got it annulled. My family doesn't know about it either."

That takes my brain a few seconds to process. "Wait, your family doesn't know you were married? How did you keep it from them?" I ask. It's hard to imagine me knowing something that intimate about Evie when I've always thought she was so close to her older brother, Drew.

"I was at college and one of my best guy friends didn't want to marry the woman his parents were hoping to connect him with. I'd had a crush on the guy for at least two semesters and then he came to me one day with flowers. We started dating and I was so excited about the whole thing. When he proposed and then said we needed to keep it quiet for a bit, I didn't think anything of it.

"We decided to elope and when his parents found out, they

made us get an annulment. Turns out he didn't really love me, but I was better than the alternative."

Hillary and I reached for Evie, pulling her into a fierce hug. This house must be doing something to me because I haven't had this much body contact with other people in a long time. First hugging Trey and now my roommates. As long as my chocolate obsession sticks around, I'll know I haven't been brainwashed or abducted.

"I shouldn't be the one complaining over here," I say, sniffling. It's crazy that I spent most of my life not having many friends who were girls and now I'm so invested in the lives of my roommates.

"Well, my fiancé didn't leave me for a Thai princess, so I automatically lose that argument." Hillary gives me a look.

They must've already spoken about Donovan because Evie doesn't look fazed.

"Yeah, well, that's about how my luck goes. It's why I'm not holding out much hope for anything with Trey. There will probably be some girl to turn his head during this adventure."

"Let's hope not," Hillary says. "Jack says you are probably the best thing for him."

I turn to level my gaze at her. "Since when did you start talking to Jack again?" I say, grinning. Jack and Hillary had been friends long before I entered the picture. I'd only known him by name until she saw him at the hockey game a few weeks ago.

"Since I figured I needed to mend all the ties I'd broken when I took off to another country. He's still mad at me, but at least I feel better about it."

"But why were Trey and I brought up in the same conversation? Please tell me you aren't the weak link." I narrow my gaze at her, the fight or flight response kicking in now.

Hillary smiles. "I told him that sending you home with Trey is probably the lamest consequence he's ever given someone for a bet. His reasoning was that it could've sparked something more."

Great. I don't need Trey's friends conspiring to get us together. That's like being five feet from an empty net and missing wide. Not going to happen.

23

KENZIE

I hate this. Why did I say yes?

Because it's getting harder and harder to say no to Trey. And because any time I spend with him is better than not spending time with him. I'm like the desert in search of rain and that man is a tall drink of water.

It's been an hour since my makeup and confessional session with Hillary and Evie, and I keep thinking about what Hillary said about Jack trying to set us up. A tiny flicker of hope burns in my chest that someone else could see the two of us working out.

But now I'm stuck in this contract for the docuseries. Chances of me telling Trey about my crush are .00001 on the possibility scale.

We're out in the middle of Boston Common and there's quite the production of people setting everything up. Camera crews, people up in trees, as well as a few of them working on one of the swan boats.

"Ready?" Trey asks, shifting from one foot to the other. It's hard to see it, but I think he's nervous too.

"I guess. I mean, it's not often I'm matched with someone for an actual date."

Truth there. My own judge of character has led me to some pretty rough situations in the past. I hate crying, but sometimes it is so cathartic that I can't help myself. But I have to remember Meg's words that I'd accidentally picked men who weren't even close to a match for me.

"Same." Trey focuses on the camera crew setting up around us.

Samantha walks up in a tight-fitting power suit. "It's good to see you two again. Your lips look much better this time, Kenzie." She reaches out her hand to shake and I'm surprised she remembers my name at all.

"Uh, thanks," I say. Just the tip of awkward for today.

"The rundown is that we'll be setting you up with mics. Our crew has already planted cameras wherever they can. If you don't want it on camera, don't say or do it."

Guess who didn't think about all that went into filming a series before signing up? Me, raising my hand all the way up.

I turn to Trey, suddenly worried. If something is wrong, my face is going to show it. He's over there nodding like he'll get participation points in school.

Traitor.

Then again, this is his contract too and I hadn't noticed the eagerness before. The guy is serious about settling down.

If only it could be with me.

I shake my head. He's here to find his perfect someone, the one who can look good on his arm when he's out and about for events. Someone who'll look perfect while pregnant and juggling their 2.5 kids. I'm jealous and it hasn't even happened yet.

It doesn't take long for the technicians to give us the mic packs and get busy with one of the boats on the water. There is a line the size of Texas waiting their turn for these boats and we're commandeering one for at least the next hour.

Someone comes up and starts brushing me with makeup and I wriggle away, not needing my skin to break out with unknown products. Sure, I sound like a snob at this point but I've done a lot of work to get rid of the acne that plagued my teen years. I'd hate to have that problem spiral out of control and not be able to do the next several dates.

"I'm good, thank you. I promise I applied my own makeup before coming here." I take a step back and grumble.

"You look really good," Trey says. His eyes widen and he says, "Not that you don't normally look good, because you do. I, uh, I'm just going to shut my mouth now."

Even for all the information I've known about Trey, it's still nice to see that he has his quirks too. Seeing him all flustered makes my heart pitter-patter even more.

Because as much torture as this is, I'd rather be here, seeing his interactions with the women he's matched with than waiting and trying to get details from him later without seeming overly interested. All because we're *friends*. Ugh, I hate that word in this context.

"Okay, here's how the scene will play out. You'll both meet your date over there by the big tree and then we'll have you wait in the front of the line for a minute or two. You can chat and get to know one another before getting on the boat. We'll have people all over the route getting different shots of the four of you. After the ride is over, you'll get in two cars we have prepped to head to dinner."

"Sounds good," Trey says. I can only nod. The woman walks away, yelling at several other people with camera equipment.

Trey turns to me and says, "How are you doing? Are you okay?"

"I'll survive."

Meg walks up from behind Trey and says, "Okay, team.

Sorry I was late. Parker had a client stay longer and a baby isn't the best idea to bring around cameras. Did they fill you in on everything?"

"Just that we'll see our dates in a few minutes," Trey said.

"How did they pick which date we go on first?" I ask, suddenly curious. "Did they just pull the names out of a hat?"

"We're starting from the bottom going up, so we matched you with a few of your lesser candidates first," Meg says coming from my side.

"Lesser candidates?" Trey and I say at the same time.

"That's the wrong word for it. They're like an 85% match."

That makes me feel a bit better. I'm struggling with the idea that I'm going to match with a guy who likes two things that are foreign to me. I may not know how to cook, but I do know how to eat. Maybe this will be a good thing.

I turn, trying to take deep breaths. I'm doing this to challenge my fears about dating. And to help Trey, who is looking as cool as a cucumber, despite his rambling a minute or two ago.

Dating this way is not going to give me nightmares. I try to convince myself it's true, but my heart knows I'm lying.

Trey must have seen the freaking out going on in my head because he moves a step closer, leaning over to whisper. "Breathe. If you need to back out, you can."

He lightly touches my back and I inhale, trying to get anything in my brain to clear. Thirteen-year-old me would be over the moon right now.

Until I remember we're on a date with different people.

"I think we're ready," one of the crew says.

I groan inwardly. Here goes nothing.

24

TREY

I'm regretting the decision to rope Kenzie into this. Her knuckles are white, and I'm worried she's either going into a comatose state or will run away screaming that she never signed up for something like this. Which she totally did but I convinced her.

The crew positions us next to a large tree and a minute later, two people start walking in our direction. I elbow Kenzie.

"I think they are our dates."

She gives a pained smile, and I want to grab her wrist to keep her from taking off, but remember the cameras. I'm supposed to be on a date with the woman coming toward me, not worrying about the one next to me, even though she smells like apple pie. My favorite.

My date is smiling as she walks toward us, but for some reason I'm sizing up the guy like I'm Kenzie's protector.

He looks a bit nerdy, wearing suspenders and a bow tie, but he's not bad looking. What will Kenzie think?

"Hi, I'm Whitney," the woman says. I turn back to her and stick out my hand, but she rushes forward and gives me a hug around the middle. I have to lean my head back so she won't try to kiss me. Not that I'm against kissing, but I don't need that five seconds after meeting. Or on camera.

"It's good to meet you, Whitney. Um, I'm Trey." And then my brain goes blank. Okay, that's a lie. I'm actually trying to hear what's going on in the conversation next to me.

"Uh, thanks for coming today?" Kenzie says, and I have to hold in a laugh. The girl is stiff as a board.

"Loosen up. Keep talking to your date," I hear through an earpiece. I'm getting personal coaching too? I didn't know they were going to do that when we got set up with the microphones.

"Let's get in line, shall we?" I say, waving toward the dock for the boats.

Whitney slips her hand into mine and I can already feel the sweat beginning.

"So, I read you're from Cleveland. What brought you to Beantown?"

She frowns and looks up at me. "Beantown?"

"Sorry, that's a nickname we use for Boston."

She laughs and I paste on a smile at the shrill sound. Yeah, I don't know if I'll survive the boat ride, let alone dinner after. Did they mix up the person I was supposed to be with?

"I came here for college and got a job at the Prudential Center. I'm from a small town originally and this is so much better than I could've imagined. There's always something to do and restaurants to try out. With a crowd as big as the city, they don't know every intimate detail of my life, which is refreshing."

And now I feel bad. "I can understand that somewhat. I grew up here but with my job, it seems like everyone knows the big news before I do in my life."

We wait behind one of the groups who are getting on the swan boats. I turn, trying to hear, and include, Kenzie and her date.

He seems to be in a monologue state, talking about the fearless empire and the difference between the colors of the light sabers.

"I still can't believe you've never watched the movies, Kenzie," he says. "We should plan a day and binge-watch all of them."

She gives him wide eyes. "Aren't there nine?"

"Yes, but there are also a few shows, like The Mandalorian and Boba Fett. Those have several episodes. It would probably take an entire weekend to watch straight through."

She gives him a small smile. "I can't usually last for two movies in a row. Maybe breaking it up over several days would be better for me." Facts. We made it through *Hitch* and part of *She's the Man* before she had to get up and move around.

Is she actually agreeing to watch the movies with him?

"The Star Wars franchise is so complex," Whitney says, now interested in the conversation.

I've watched all the movies the guy is talking about but that was in support of my little sister. She has been obsessed since she was young and it's all about the bonding time. Well, it's usually her trying to explain why some small line is important while I smile and nod like I understand.

It's our turn to board so I take a step in front of Whitney to get in the boat and hopefully help her in. Instead, she tries to push past me and we nearly fall off the ledge and into the water.

"Let me help you in," I say, trying to keep my calm.

Whitney smiles brightly. "Oh, sorry about that." She glances down to where my hands are grasping her upper arms and is practically beaming at this point.

I let go and step into the boat, making sure to keep one foot on the shore to hold it as steady as possible. I'm not sure why the people who run the boat couldn't help me with that much. Then again, I'm just glad I'm not soaking wet right now.

Whitney settles into a seat and I turn, reaching out for Kenzie's hand. She shakes her head. "I'm good."

"I don't care if you're good," I say, trying to give her a look of warning. "My mother taught me some manners."

Finally, she reaches out and touches my hand, the surprising softness throwing me off. Sure, I held her hand the other day, but I was more focused on her physical health. The zing of excitement has me backing up a bit, almost losing my grip of the boat.

Once she's settled in behind Whitney, I turn to head over to the seat by my date.

"If you don't mind, I'm a little nervous of boats," Kenzie's date says. I turn to see his hand outstretched, as though he wants me to help him in.

I reach out for his forearm and help him into the boat. Kenzie is trying to keep a smile from forming and that makes it that much harder for me to keep a straight face.

The ride begins and I remember a time my mother brought all us kids down here to go on the swan boats. I'd been a pill about it, not wanting to be seen by my friends doing something as girly as this. Yet, here I am and I can guarantee that my friend group will be watching this docuseries, pointing out all the little things I'm doing wrong and making fun of me for months. I probably should've rethought my part in this.

"What do you like to do for fun?" I ask Whitney. If we're filming, it will be better to look interested and engaged, even though I wish I were curled up on my couch watching a movie. As Kenzie pointed out earlier though, I'd have to hook the TV up to do that.

"I love crafting. I've been doing a craft blog for the past several years and finally set up a shop where I can sell some of the things I've made. My mom was getting frustrated at all the space my pieces were taking up in the basement."

I nod. "I can relate to that. My mom was excited to get rid of all the stuff she'd saved for me over the past twenty-eight years. I have several totes stacked up in my garage and guest bedroom."

"Yeah, and his organizer is still trying to figure out what to do with them," Kenzie says from behind us.

Turning, I say, "Yeah, maybe she needs some monetary compensation. She's doing a lot to help me right now."

Kenzie rolls her eyes but I can see a glimmer of a smile behind the mask.

We make small talk until we get to the middle of the ride. Whitney is a little intense, but she's good at conversations, which makes the ride a little easier. I haven't checked on Kenzie and Mr. Vader in a while but I don't have to.

"I'm sorry, I said I'm not a really touchy person." I turn to see that Kenzie has scooted over to the edge of the boat.

Mr. Vader is smiling at her. "I've never held someone's hand. Won't you let me do that, just for the rest of the ride?"

Kenzie stands up, as if she's going to be able to get away from him that way. Vader dude reaches out and touches her fingertips. As if seeing it in slow motion, she rips her hands out of the way, but the movement propels her backward and into the water.

Seconds tick by and there's no sign of her coming up for air. I have Whitney switch me seats, so I can lean over to see. The water is opaque, making it difficult to see anything. Taking a deep breath, I jump in, hitting the bottom a lot sooner than I'd planned. Instead of being submerged in the water, it's waist high.

I bend over, wondering if I just swing my arms through the water if I'll find her. Maybe she hit her head and is unconscious? I take a few tentative steps to where she fell in and don't feel anything. A few more steps and the panic sets in.

"No jumping out of the boats," the boat conductor yells, frowning at me.

"What are you doing?" Whitney asks, leaning over the side.

"Making sure Kenzie is all right." This is too shallow to know if I need to worry about her ability to swim.

Just then, Kenzie breaks the surface, causing me to jump back in surprise.

I trip over a rock and start to go down when Kenzie leans forward and pulls me back up. We're close, the water spilling off her causing the mascara to run. I stand up and reach forward, using my thumbs to wipe at the black smears.

"What are you doing?" Kenzie asks, in a harsh whisper. She uses her hands to push the hair out of her face.

"I wasn't sure if you knew how to swim."

Kenzie stands up and gives me a disbelieving look. "The water is all of three feet."

"Trey, you're all wet. What are we going to do now?" Whitney asks. The boat is five feet past Kenzie and I now.

The driver of the boat keeps pedaling. "Get out of the water and meet over by the dock. We have some towels in there to dry off with."

The boat continues on, and Whitney and Mr. Vader turn to look at us like we've lost our minds. I'm not going to deny that.

25

KENZIE

If I wasn't already in the water, I'd be jumping in right now.

Having Trey that close, touching me so intimately has every nerve ending in my face wanting more. A cameraman pops out from behind one of the trees, the camera aimed at us.

"We should probably get out of the water," I say, turning away from Trey. I try to keep my cool and wait for more instructions to come through the ear piece. But there isn't even a faint buzz. Did I kill the microphone when I fell into the pond? Please say yes.

"I'm surprised you don't like to be touched so much that you fell in the water," Trey says from behind me.

I push forward and climb out of the pond to sit on the grassy side. "Did you see that guy's hands? He had a huge wart on his palm and then a few all over his fingers. I don't need to get that virus from a guy I just met."

Trey leans back in the grass and laughs.

"What?" I ask, laying back as well.

"There is never a dull moment with you around, Kenz."

"That's how I like it," I say, trying not to register the shiver that goes through my body when he says my name like that. Like we've known each other forever.

A buzzing sound in my ear turns into someone talking. "We're still on. We should probably hurry back to the dock." I hop up and start walking that direction.

Trey shakes his head. "No, you're worried about Wart Vader."

"I can't believe you called him that," I say, laughing so hard I snort. "It fits, though."

We start running toward the beginning of the ride, and I'm grateful for the humid summer air or else I'd be freezing.

"So much for not falling in the water, huh?" he says, hitting my arm with his elbow.

"I wasn't the one who made you fall in. You did that all on your own." I laugh a bit before realizing how he's looking at me. Almost like this is the first time he's seen the real me.

"True. Now if anyone asks me how deep the pond is, I'll tell them three feet."

I give him a lopsided grin and say, "I doubt many people care."

Laughing, Trey says, "I'll make sure they care."

We make it back to the dock and I can't get his nickname for my date out of my head.

Instead of our dates worrying about us, they're standing closely, talking animatedly about something.

Trey and I turn to each other. "Star Wars."

"I can't compete with that," I say.

"Me either."

"Cut!" rings out and we both turn, trying to figure out what's going on.

One of the camera crew comes out from behind one of the bushes toward us. "You look disgusting," he says, giving us a once over. "We'll have to postpone the rest of this date until the two of you have dried yourselves off."

"I don't know if this date is worth salvaging," Trey says, pointing to the couple behind us. "I think a match was made, just not the one on the schedule."

I laugh at his words since he's trying to be so serious. The camera guy cuts me a look and I stop and straighten, like I'm going to be punished with a seriously long cardio workout.

"I'll have to call my boss. For now, go home and change."

I turn to say goodbye to Wart Vader and it takes three tries to get his attention. "It was good to meet you."

"Thank you for helping me meet Whitney. I'm sorry things didn't work out between us."

I glance down and see he's holding her hand. Cringe. "No problem. Good luck with everything." I can't help but squirm at the delayed results of that hand holding session.

Water is still dripping from all my clothes and my hair, so I try to squeeze some of it out.

"Looks like you dodged a bullet," Trey says, twisting his shirt to let out a steady waterfall. Of course, that means I can see some of his skin underneath, and I have to look away before I get caught staring. I mean, my chances are slim with this guy. Even if there was some chemistry happening a few moments ago. Too bad it was in stinky water.

Even though today's date bombed, there are still three more to go.

"Yeah, on a few levels. I'll see you later. I took the train here."

"What are you doing tonight?" Trey asks and I stop in my tracks. Did I hear him correctly? Those kinds of words usually lead to what is normally termed a date.

I shrug. "I'm not sure now. I mean, we were supposed to be eating with our respective dates, right? I could get a few hours of work in."

"Why don't you come to my house and we'll order food? Then you can walk me through your process of organization."

The temptation is strong. Of course, why wouldn't I want to go hang out at his house and ogle him while trying to earn a paycheck.

"I'm soaked."

"Me too. I took an Uber here. Why don't I call us a ride to take you home to change and then you can come back? I had some ideas I wanted to run by you."

He's trying awfully hard to get me to his house. And then he takes a step forward, making my breath hitch. He lifts his hands into my line of sight and gives me a small smile.

I give him a strange look. "What are you doing?"

"Showing you that there are no warts on my person." He starts laughing and I join in half-heartedly.

"Trey, you're my boss. I don't think holding hands is necessary." Even though I would love to check that one off my list. Again.

He sighs. "I know, I was just making a joke. You won't have to worry about picking them up from me."

"Fine, it will be good to make some progress on your house. There's no way I'm up for the torture that is my dad's house today."

"Chinese okay?"

"Now you're speaking my language," I say, grinning.

He pulls out his phone, which somehow didn't get hit by the water because he's taller than me. Once he's off the phone, he says, "Should just be five minutes. She's close."

"Who's close?" All I need is the continued torture of watching him with yet another woman.

"My sister."

What was I thinking?

Moms are usually more open to any women in their son's life. The sisters are the ones who'll either breathe fear into the potential prospect, or report back to the mom everything she sees. I should've never agreed to a work dinner.

26

TREY

Okay, it's not my proudest moment, but I figured she wouldn't want to ride home with one of her roommates or one of my good friends. There's too much to tell on that front and I don't need my friends pointing out how well we click together. Because I'm already feeling that.

Payton is Switzerland in that regard, except she's my sister and she won't be able to keep her mouth shut when she gets home. It's worth the risk though.

"Our chariot awaits, m'lady," I say, trying to ease Kenzie into the fact that we're basically being chaperoned by my sister, the Uber/Lyft driver. At least the car is clean when we get in.

"Trey, welcome to the speed wagon. And who's your beautiful friend?" Payton gives me a few looks and I know what she's thinking. To be honest, I might've been thinking similar thoughts while in the water, I just don't need anyone scaring Kenzie away.

"I'm Kenzie, Kenzie Sullivan. I'm the reason we're wet." She pauses and then says, "And by that, I mean I fell into the water and Trey here thought I was drowning."

Payton shakes her head. "Dear brother, don't you know that the pond is like three feet deep?"

I purse my lips as Kenzie gives me a smug look. "Okay, I see your point," I say, referencing her comment that no one would care about knowing the depth of the pond. Am I the only one in Boston who didn't know this most random of facts?

"Where to, friendlies?" It's not hard to see that Payton is eating this up, filing every detail away for when she gets home later. I'll have to pay her off or something so she doesn't tell Mom.

"My place," Kenzie and I say at the same time.

"Sorry, we'll go to her house first," I say, pointing to Kenzie.

"That way I can get showered and then get back to work on your house," Kenzie says, looking at me with an expression I can't quite read.

Payton pulls out into traffic. "Oh, are you the one organizing Trey's place?" Kenzie nods and I can see mischief in Payton's eyes as she looks back at me through the rearview mirror.

Kenzie gives her directions, but Payton leans forward and turns up the music, pretending to rock out as she drives the opposite way.

"Payton," I say, leaning forward so she can hear me. "What are you doing?"

She reaches back with her hand and pats me on the cheek with her palm, smiling wide. "Just helping you out there, bro."

I grimace, turning to Kenzie and pleading forgiveness with a look. Payton parks in my driveway and finally turns down the music.

"Have fun you two. Let me know if I can be your ride again sometime." We get out of the car and she rolls down the passenger side window and calls out, "You should come to family dinner sometime. I'm sure Trey would love to introduce you to everyone."

And heat rises to my face. One of my friends would've been better than this.

"Sorry about her," I say, trying to break whatever weird tension is between us now. "She is kind of a free spirit and there's no controlling what she'll say or do."

"Well, this way I don't have to take the train to get here. I just wish I didn't smell like a pond." She leans over and takes a sniff of her shirt. From her scrunched nose and pinched lips, I take it the smell is awful.

I open the door and wave for her to enter. "I've got a shower and you probably know where my clothes are better than I do at this point. Help yourself to whatever is comfortable or fits."

Her eyes look glassy for a moment and I'm not exactly sure what that's about.

"I think I'll be okay," she says, wrapping her arms around her middle.

"Are you sure you're going to survive whatever stench made you make that face?"

She sighs. "You're right. I'd make the whole place stink. Do you mind if I get in right now?"

"Sure thing. Use the master shower. You know where all the things are anyway." She disappears into the master bathroom and I stand still, thinking about the events that got us here.

And now the nerves set in. What do I do while I wait for a woman to leave my shower? Instead of letting myself dwell on what happens when she's in the shower, I glance around at the mess. I left my cereal bowl out on the counter and the last half of the jug of milk. A quick smell test tells me that it's beyond hope, so I pour it down the drain.

It's a race to get as much cleaned up as possible before she comes out of the bathroom.

I'm just starting a load of laundry when I see her walk out, wearing a pair of basketball shorts with the waistband folded over a couple times and then the Breeze shirt I'd worn the other day, the one that looked like a crop top on me. It barely touches the top of the waistband of the shorts and I just realize how long I've been staring at her middle.

"Um, how was the shower?"

She uses her hands and flicks some of the water out of her hair, causing my brain to malfunction as I watch her.

"I love the house I live in, but that shower is now on my future home bucket list," she says, pointing her thumb behind her. "There's so much room." She's smiling and again I'm caught on how amazing her eyes are and her smile.

I don't know why I was so persistent about her coming over tonight, but I didn't want to be alone. And who better to dissect the odd date with me than the person who was there for it. That's the reason, I keep telling myself, not that I'm feeling drawn to her all of a sudden.

"It's one of my favorite things in the house," I say. I motion for her to take a seat on the couch and it all seems so formal. Kenzie has been in this house several times to work on stuff and now I'm acting like a teenager with a new crush, all awkward and stiff.

"Okay, do you want to order the Chinese?" she asks. "I can get started on some of the things I've been meaning to get to since the last time I was here."

"Chinese should be here soon. I'm going to take a shower and then I'll come help?" Why it's a question, I don't know. Maybe I need to knock my head into the wall or something to get out of this weird state I'm in.

Kenzie nods. "Awesome."

I head into the shower, grateful for the spray of the water to keep me focused. The surge of feelings for Kenzie is making me wonder if we've spent too much time together or if there is something there that I've been missing. But how do I navigate testing the waters when we have to go on three more dates with other people?

27

KENZIE

The first thing I tackle while he's gone is the TV. I'm not sure it's completely normal for a guy not to have that set up as the first thing once he moves in. I had to do this in the Spice House when I first moved in. And just about everywhere else I've lived.

I've got it placed up on the cabinet set he's got in the front room and all the channels are working. It will be better on the wall, but there are only so many things I can do by myself safely.

"Wow, you got it to work?" Trey asks, pulling a t-shirt down over his oh-so-gorgeous chest and it takes me a few extra seconds to answer.

"Yeah, it's not that hard." I gesture for him to move closer and give him the rundown on the controller buttons. "You should be good now. I mean, you've got the local stations anyway."

He frowns. "Is there a way you can connect to some of the streaming services?"

"Trey Hatch, do you not know how to do that? Sorry, I shouldn't have said it like that," I say when I see him frown.

"No, you're okay. And no, I'm not sure how to do that. Any help you can give would be great." He sits down on the couch, and I sit close enough to show him what we need to do to download the apps on his smart TV and then get set up on the logins.

He lets out a small snort and says, "I bet Wart Vader would know how to do all this."

I turn to see he's picking at something on his shorts, kind of like he's embarrassed.

"Probably, but why does that matter?" I ask, surprised to see the fantasy guy I've liked for so long has real insecurities. I could be the poster girl for those after all the changes I've made, and I still wonder sometimes if it could all turn out to be a dream.

"Guys are supposed to know that kind of stuff, inherently."

I laugh, trying to decide what to say. "Trey, I've met plenty of people who don't know how to set up a TV. That doesn't make them any less of a person. I will say, though, you can find any tutorial you need on YouTube these days. When in doubt, that's where I look to figure things out."

"Thanks," he says, looking a little more cheerful. "Nice rhyme."

The doorbell rings and the smell of Chinese wafts in when Trey opens the door. "Sorry, I didn't really ask what you like. I'm a fan of the sweet and sour chicken and broccoli beef."

"If you got chow mien noodles, you'll have picked the perfect meal." I walk over to the cabinet and neither of the two plates are in the cupboard. "Did you break your last two plates?"

"No," Trey says, unpacking the plastic bag the food came in. "They're in the dishwasher."

I lean my hip against the counter, trying to get him to look me in the eye. We haven't been this close in all of a couple hours and I'm okay with the lack of distance. "You don't have to speed clean when I'm around, you know."

He gives me the cutest side-eye slight grin I've ever seen and says, "I didn't speed clean, it was more of a competition with myself to see how much I could get done before you got out of the shower."

I roll my eyes and open the dishwasher to see that there are still dribbles of water on the plates. I grab the one dish towel from where I'd placed it in the drawer while unpacking the kitchen a few days before.

Once the plates are wiped dry, I place them across the counter to where the bar stools sit. I get out the forks and Trey already has his mismatched cups filled with ice and water. As I look at the scene before me, this isn't a fancy dinner, but the way we work together to prepare all the things makes it feel like we're in a relationship.

Or a friendlyship.

I'd prefer to think of it as the first one even though that's not good for my mental health.

The ambience is quiet but comfortable as we both pile food onto our plates. At one point, Trey grins, looking down at my portions.

"What? Have you never seen a woman eat before?" I say dryly.

"Only on rare occurrences. But I'd prefer it this way," he says, motioning between his plate and mine. "Otherwise, I get self-conscious about looking like a pig."

I tilt my head a bit to study him better. "Hmm, I didn't realize some guys felt like that."

"What do you think of the dating docuseries so far?" he asks, watching me closely.

"I'm good. Just nervous about what the next few dates will bring, you know? I mean, that guy–"

"Wart Vader," Trey adds.

I smile, trying to keep it together as I picture the whole scene from earlier. "He seemed nice, but there were several signs that just pushed me away. The immediate hand holding was a bright red flag. PDA isn't my favorite."

"You haven't had a problem hugging me. Did something happen in your past that made you avoid any kind of touching?"

I'm surprised he noticed. "I had a boyfriend, ex-fiancé actually, who was over the top with affection."

Trey's attention seems to perk up the minute I mention "ex-fiancé."

"So, you're against it because of him?"

I finally look up, locking eyes with him. "I don't know if I can trust it, you know? Everyone says not to trust words but to trust actions. He proposed and then came back a couple days later for the ring, saying he was marrying a Thai princess."

Trey blinked several times, as if trying to decide if I'm lying or not. "Wait, what?"

I let out a small laugh. "Yep, a real-life Thai princess. Like, how can a girl compete with that? I'm already different because I love sports and extreme activities, and I'm definitely not royal." The laugh turns into a small cry and I bury my head in my arms for a moment.

"Uh, are you okay?" Trey asks, poking my shoulder.

"I'll be fine. I'm just sick of being passed over." I stab a piece of broccoli with my fork before taking a big bite. "Then again, I did the same thing to my date today."

Trey frowns, patting my shoulder for a moment. "Sorry, I'm not good with tears even though I have sisters."

His somber admission hits a chord with me and I nearly choke on the broccoli. He slaps my back, which helps dislodge things a bit. Not the romantic scene I've pictured a few times.

"How's that Chinese food treating you?" he asks with a grin.

"Chinese always helps me figure life out."

He nods. "I didn't think there was that much to it. You'll have to show me your ways, Jedi."

I give a half-hearted laugh. "Just because I went on one date with a Star Wars fan doesn't mean I'm ready to watch it. Or take nicknames from it. Then again, we could call you Pond Boy or something like that."

We chat for a bit, eating the food in front of us. Once we clean up the mess and head into the living room, we sit on the couch and I pull out my laptop. I find the website for my favorite furniture store. Not that I have a whole lot of experience buying pieces from there, but the reviews are all amazing and it's on my someday list.

"Okay, I want you to take a look at these options. We'll need a lot to go in the guest bedroom, and several shelving units for your garage to hold all the totes, but those are some of the thoughts I had." I hand him the laptop and stand up.

"Where are you going?" he asks, looking panicked like I'm leaving him here by himself.

"I figured the first thing to get done was to mount your TV." I walk over to a box and pull out a small toolset I'd seen the other day.

"You know how to do that?" he asks, curious.

Flashing him a knowing smile, I say, "I've done it a few times."

He looks even more guilty than he did about the TV setup. "I never really needed to. I'd just leave it there long enough and one of my roommates would set it up. Except for that plan backfired since I don't have any roommates."

"You focus on picking the furniture and I'll start working on this. When I need your help to lift the TV, I'll ask."

"Ahh, so you do know how to ask for help then?" he asks with a smirk. My brain goes back to the boat earlier today when I insisted I could get in by myself.

"Once in a blue moon."

It takes about twenty minutes to get everything set up and mounted to the wall. I've gathered all the extra cords from his gaming units and tried to hide them as much as possible.

"Did you order anything?" I ask, sitting down next to him.

He shakes his head. "There are things I like, but I'm worried that if I order without seeing and feeling, that I'll regret it. What if we go to a store and try them out?"

Shopping with Trey would be a whole trip. "Yeah, we can do that. We'll have to work around the filming schedule. What about your workouts and preseason stuff?"

He waves a hand in the air. "I can do those whenever. The offseason is when my schedule is the most flexible."

"Okay, I'm going to head out. Let's order the garage shelving units because those are standard. We're going to need those here soon so we can start moving around the totes and opening the space." I pause to think about anything else we'll need. "Then I'll have to schedule some time for the container store to find the odds and ends."

"Just let me know. I might be able to drive out there with you." He pauses, watching as I put away the few tools I used on the mount. "Wait, let me drive you home."

"I'll be okay," I say. I stow my laptop in the bag.

Trey slips on shoes and grabs his keys from a basket by the door. "I've got you. Did you grab your clothes?"

I'd almost totally forgotten that I'm wearing Trey's clothes. "Do you mind if I return these to you later?" I ask, pointing to the t-shirt and shorts.

"For sure. I don't want you getting a cold from wearing your wet stuff again."

He grins and I'm pretty sure that the guy has me hooked and he just keeps reeling me in. Whether he knows he's doing that or not is another story.

28

TREY

"Trey, you'll be waiting here for your date, Melissa. Then we'll take some shots of you walking into the aquarium. She'll be here in about five minutes."

"Wait, where's Kenzie?" I ask. Samantha is studying the clipboard in front of her and glances up as if she just now heard me.

"Kenzie and her date are at the Museum of Fine Art today." She lifts her arm to glance at the watch on her wrist. "They should be starting in about an hour."

My stomach sinks. I guess I didn't really ask and only assumed that we would be together for every date we went on. "Can I ask why we didn't have another double date?"

"The last one you went on together was a disaster."

"Are you kidding?" I say, trying to keep from laughing at the ridiculousness of the two of us dunked in water. "You still made a match with Whitney and W–the other guy."

Samantha takes a step forward, her gaze intense as she speaks. "Is there something between the two of you?"

That was kind of a complicated question. "Well, she, uh, is organizing my house. And we're friends." Why does that word taste so bitter on my tongue? After the time we've spent together, it's like I want to keep her next to me just to see her reaction to things. And the fact that she doesn't put me down because of skills I don't have is commendable.

"You're friends?" Samantha says, looking as though she doesn't believe me.

"Yeah, I don't do well with cameras and I completely forgot about them on the last date because she was there."

"Probably because you were waterlogged from the pond water." She reaches up and touches her ear, nodding at something I can't hear. "Yeah, we're ready." She turns to me and says, "We're starting. Just relax and have fun on the date."

I'd been so excited that the date would be at the aquarium and hadn't thought to text Kenzie to meet up before. Lesson learned.

Me: They split us up today. 😟

Kenzie: What? You're not going to be there to question the art choices?

I grin, knowing that would've been exactly how it played out.

Me: I'm waiting at the aquarium. Should we meet at my house tonight and do a recap?

There isn't a response for several moments. A sound in my ear causes me to glance up and see a woman walking toward me—Melissa, who loves books and traveling.

"Hi," I say, reaching out my hand to shake. Instead, she keeps moving and wraps her arms around me in a big hug. What is it with these women that make them so informal? It took several times for Kenzie to come close enough for a hug. And now, I'm wishing it was Kenzie I'm holding and not feeling the rise of nerves from the several cameras pointed toward us.

"It's nice to meet you, Trey. I'm a huge fan," Melissa says.

"That's cool," I say. Usually when women say that, I have to figure out their true intentions. "Do you watch a lot of hockey?"

She nods. "My brothers and dad have been a huge fan of the Breeze for most of my life. I still don't understand how icing the puck works, but I understand most of the rules."

I smile, nodding. "It took me a while to figure out icing too. What are some of your favorite things to do?" I need to keep the conversation going and not focus on the cameras I can see out of the corner of my eye.

"I actually do a lot of reading. I'm a bookstagrammer and spend a lot of time creating content for that when I'm not reading."

"So, you post about the books you read on social media? Are there a lot of people who respond to those?"

Melissa grins. "There is quite the community of book loving fans out there. One lady messaged me once that I need to read more so I can get out recommendations faster. She reads like two books a day."

"That's crazy," I say. "Now I feel like a slacker. It's been a while since I've read a book I've loved." Probably since high school at least. I wonder if Kenzie likes to read. She's like the Energizer Bunny and can barely sit still for a movie, let alone reading a book that would take multiple hours.

"What's your favorite type of books?" she asks as we start walking toward the aquarium.

"Great question," I say, trying to think back to those days. "I mean, I enjoy a good mystery, but that's because I watch a lot of detective shows."

Melissa nods. "That still translates to books. I read mostly romance, but it would be good to venture out and read something different. We should pick a book and read it together."

What in the first date book club?

"I can't make any promises on that. Preseason training starts soon and once we get going, I'm mostly watching film from our games as well as our opponents."

Her smile falls a bit and I feel bad. Glancing around, I'm excited to see what's here.

"Where do you want to start?" I ask.

"How about the tropical fish? Those are my favorite."

I nod, wishing we were seeing the bigger sea animals instead. "Turtles and sea lions next?" I ask.

"Yeah, we can do that."

We wander through the aquarium for over an hour. I'm excited about seeing the turtles and go off on several random facts about them.

"Did you know sea turtles don't retract their head and their flippers like the land ones?" I watch as two large turtles swim through the water, admiring the easy way they do it. "They can also hold their breath for over five hours."

"I take it turtles are your favorite?" Melissa asks, smiling.

Nodding, I say, "I rescued a land turtle when we went to the beach one year and that ignited my love for all turtles. What do you think of them?"

"They're cool," she says. But I can tell the excitement isn't there like it was for the fluorescent-colored fish. Understandable.

We continue heading for the devil rays. The conversation hasn't been the best, but I also haven't been trying that hard. I've been distracted wondering what Kenzie would say if she were here and wondering what her next date looks like. Would he have warts too? Or would he be the kind of guy to sweep her off her feet?

I frown, trying to picture Kenzie getting that excited about something like that. Then again, she was giddy while we watched *Hitch* the other night.

"Are you okay? I've been talking and I don't think you heard a word." Melissa raises an eyebrow and looks concerned.

"I'm fine. Sorry. I just was thinking about something. What do you want to do now?"

We've made it through the aquarium and I'm itching to dig out my phone and call Kenzie, or text her at least.

"How about we walk over to the bakery right there?" she points and I have to squint to see the name of the place.

"Sure," I say. "So, how did you decide to go through a matchmaker?" Not my best conversation starter, but hopefully it will finally break through the ice we've had throughout the aquarium.

Melissa blows out a breath. "I've been on a lot of dates, usually with people my friends or family have tried to set me up with. I know they have good intentions, but they miss the mark every single time. I figured if I could have a better assurance of having similar interests to the guy, I might as well try. What about you?"

"To be honest, I'm ready to settle down. I've achieved a lot of success and I want someone to share it with."

Her expression is unreadable so I do what I'm good at and keep talking.

"It's hard because my parents were able to meet by chance and then got married soon after. That's not as easy when my life is on the road and in and out of the city a lot."

"Marriage, huh?" Melissa says, giving a small laugh. "That's going kinda fast, don't you think?"

I turn to study her. "Are you not the marrying type?"

"I've had a lot of boyfriends who've dragged their feet when it comes to saying 'I do'. But we've only just met, so that's a little intimidating."

And of course, I messed up on something so small. Maybe I need to have someone coach me through the first several dates so I don't screw them up.

"Sorry, I don't want to give you the wrong impression. I'm not saying I've got a ring in my pocket and am going to get down on one knee right here. I guess what I'm saying is that I'm motivated to get there sooner, rather than years down the road."

We order a pastry and then sit on a bench in the sunshine.

"That's always good to know." Melissa is avoiding eye contact with me and I've officially struck out on this date. Would things have been different if Kenzie had been here to help the conversation?

Then again, she'd been engaged to someone who dumped her for a Thai princess. She'd probably have a few things to say.

We sit in silence, eating the food and I'm retracing steps to see where I went wrong. What are the characteristics that are similar between the two of us? Because it was like striking out left and right.

"Wrap it up," the ear piece says.

"Thank you for a nice time, Melissa," I say, standing. She gives me a short hug and nods.

"It was fun to hang out today. I hope everything goes well in the coming weeks." With that, she turns away and tosses her pastry wrapper in the garbage. She's gone within a minute and I'm still standing there, feeling like a heel.

I blew another chance at a match, but I don't want to settle. I want to keep the woman I'm in a relationship with in my thoughts and close to me.

Pulling out my phone, I go to text Kenzie.

What had ruined the date? The fact that I kept wondering what she was up to rather than paying attention to Melissa? Or that I'd mentioned marriage?

I'm going to say the marriage bit sealed the deal of no second date.

The biggest question is why? What is it about Kenzie that keeps pulling my thoughts in her direction?

The relatability, the dry humor. The fact that she doesn't bend over backwards to try and impress me.

Do I have feelings for Kenzie? A few seconds ticks by and I think my heart is telling me yes. Probably not the four-letter word kind of feeling, but there's something there.

Now I've got to figure out how far I'm willing to go with it and see if she even feels the same.

My phone rings with Owen's name on the screen. It's early for his call. Hopefully nothing happened.

29

KENZIE

Today's date was still on the rough spectrum. I can picture Trey's date being even cuter and more perky, while mine was a Lord of the Rings fan. I guess we're going to cover every fantasy genre out there on these dates. We went to the Museum of Fine Art and actually made it to dinner this time. It was an anticlimactic date, up until he tried to go in for a cheek kiss and I pulled out a *Matrix* move to dodge.

It was a bit much, but I can only control so much of my instincts when it comes to the opposite sex and their intentions.

And then there's Trey. I got brave and hugged him the other day, but I wouldn't mind something more when it comes to him. Except he probably had the time of his life with his second match. He's probably glad we didn't get paired up for this date. I'm sure the producers of the show are grateful too.

I could text him and casually see what he's up to, but that would be taking it too far. Then again, I could make it about the job. The stuff we ordered won't arrive until the end of the week.

Ugh, hormones are lame at this time of the month. Just because he didn't call or text doesn't mean I need to obsess over it.

Shaking my head, I refocus on my current job.

Sullivan Home Cleaning Log Day 1067.

Okay, so I don't know what day I'm on cleaning my father's home, but I know it feels at least that long. With the bits and pieces of time I've been able to spend there, it hasn't gone as quickly as I would like.

Yet, it's been good for my dad to go through the room I'm currently working on to find anything he doesn't want taken away. We've already had the dumpster emptied once, and from the look of this place, it's going to be another four or five before the house is cleaned out.

"Kenz the Benz," a familiar voice says behind me. I turn to see my oldest brother getting out of his family van. "How's it coming in there?"

"Turtle slow."

Even though Damian isn't my dad's biological son, my dad adopted him and my other two half-brothers once he married my mother.

"What brings you here?" I ask, pulling out a new mask and a pair of gloves from one of the boxes I bought yesterday.

"I figured you could use some reinforcements." He points to the curb where my other two brothers are getting out of a truck.

"You all came to help?"

Damian pulls me in for a hug and squeezes hard enough to make it difficult to breathe. "We know what it was like growing up before you came along to keep things in line. I figured we could get our hands dirty and help get this place cleaned up for Dad."

"Your hands aren't all that's going to be dirty. Take a mask and gloves. You're going to need them."

Once inside, I turn to see their collective faces, eyes wide over the mask. "He's been living like this?" Porter asks.

"This isn't even half of it. This is the kitchen after several days of cleaning." There are still some mounds of garbage and the odd broken dishwasher in the middle of the room.

They all shake their heads. "I should've checked in earlier. Dad just always asked to meet somewhere else. I never thought that he might be having trouble here." Ty's eyes are tearing up, and I get it. The emotional weight of what's happening around us is more than we could've comprehended.

"Let's get going. Dad said he was going to get gas when I got here." I start giving directions, telling my brothers where to put things and the process that will get this done the fastest. Having them here to help is a boost to my enthusiasm for the job.

We spend an hour in the kitchen and have cleaned it up to the point it's ready for a deep scrub cleaning.

"Keep us working," Damian says. "Julie knows I'll be here for as long as you need me. These guys too." He punctuates the last word with a slap to Ty's gut.

"The family room is piled high with so much stuff. I'd say we can get rid of the garbage and then we'll wait for Dad to find anything of value to him."

Porter shakes his head as we all look at the scene before us. "Are you sure there's anything valuable in there?"

"It might not look that way to us," I say, grabbing a garbage bag and picking up a bunch of used coffee cups. "From everything I've researched though, we have to ease him into the changes or else he'll revert back. We also need to convince him to see someone about this." I wave to the mess, wishing I could wave a magic wand to make it disappear.

Everyone turns to Ty. "Ty is the best option for that," Damian says, pulling down the mask for a second. His beard has to take up most of the space in the mask, probably making it hard to breathe.

"Why me?" Ty asks, his voice going high and squeaky like when he was younger. We all know secretly he's pleased.

"Because you were the one to convince him to go on that

road trip when I was in elementary, remember? I don't think he's taken an extended vacation since," I say, putting my hand on my hip.

"I've gone on vacation," Dad's voice calls out and we all jump and turn around to the back door. "Wow, there's a kitchen here." Tears well in his eyes and his lips tremble.

I walk over and take the bags from his hands, noting that it's just regular food groceries and breathe a sigh of relief. I don't want to have to hide more stuff from him.

He's visibly shaking at this point. I wrap my arms around him and pull tight, just like Damian did to me.

"Now you can cook some meals here. Or at least reheat them," Porter says.

We all laugh at that. None of us were blessed with the ability to cook. Damian snagged himself a wife who knows the ins and outs of the kitchen and can make a decent meal out of a handful of ingredients. Porter and Ty are still single but definitely ready to mingle, as Porter always says.

"How about we keep this going in here, Dad? The boys said they have time to help more tonight. What do you want to keep?"

Instead, Dad is distracted as he glances around the kitchen. "I haven't seen this linoleum for at least six years."

"You might want to get that torn out," Ty says. Damian and Porter hit him so he'll be quiet.

"One thing at a time, boys," I say, clucking as if I'm their mama bird.

We walk into the living room, my arm gently guiding my father forward. "It looks like we have a few tons of clothes and knickknacks. Books and magazines. Why don't you go through and find your favorites, Dad? I'll let the boys haul out the trash and then we can make a donation pile."

"You're going to give it all away?" he asks, turning to me with an expression that reminds me of a young child.

Shaking my head, I say, "No, we'll just give away the things that are still usable to people who can use it."

Something about that settles him and he nods. While Dad peruses through the stack of books, the four of us kids are pulling up more and more garbage. At least this is mostly plastic wrapping and paper tags that have been deposited on the floor. I don't think I'll ever get the stench of rotten meat out of my nostrils after cleaning out the fridge this morning. I'll take this cleaning any day.

"You're pretty awesome, Kenz," Damian says from my side.

"Well, a girl has to start somewhere with her entrepreneurial endeavors. So, if you know of people who want some organization in their life, pass them my name."

"I'll hire you," Porter says. "My apartment is tiny and needs all the help it can get."

My heart warms at the thought my family is coming together to support me on this new venture. "It will be a couple weeks but I can give you the family discount."

"Who else do you have?" Damian asks.

"Dad hired me but I'm not going to charge him. And I'm organizing Trey Hatch's home."

"You are working at Trey's house? Does he have a restraining order against you yet?" Ty jokes. Just another reason why I don't share feelings that often. I spent all my growing up years going through the teasing and torture of older brothers.

I hit him with my fist, not wanting to go into that. "Of course not. I've never been a stalker and he's my client—I'm a professional."

Porter hefts the garbage bag into the dumpster and it looks like that one had more than just papers in it. "Aren't you doing some kind of dating show? I think Dad said something about it the other day."

How in the blazes did my dad find out about the docuseries?

"No, it's not a dating show. Well, kind of. They're just trying to show the process of matchmaking." From their smirks, I don't even want to go into the details.

"How have your dates been so far?" Porter asks.

"They seem like nice guys. The first one ended up falling for Trey's date."

Damian stares at me. "Wait, what?"

"Trey is doing the docuseries too?" Ty asks.

"Technically, I'm not supposed to say anything about it yet, but yes, Trey is one of the people getting matched on the show."

Damian, Porter, and Ty all lean in, ridiculous grins on their face. "So, any chance you could get matched up with Trey?"

Shaking my head, I say, "I doubt it. There are like eight main daters and we go on dates with people we've matched with. That would be kind of weird because I'm working for him right now."

"I don't think that hinders things when it comes to relationships," Ty says, leaning against the dumpster. "Why are we standing here? It smells awful."

We all chuckle and move back inside. Dad announces he's got what he wants.

Another three hours and I'm exhausted. We make good progress in the bedroom and I finally feel like I can breathe inside again. There is going to be a group of people who'll never have to buy clothes again with the amount we're going to donate.

"I've got to head out," Ty says, giving me a hug around the middle and lifting so my feet are flailing off the ground. "Let us know if you need help again, sis. See you at the game tonight?"

"I almost forgot we play tonight. Will you make sure to drop that off at the donation place on your way?" I ask, pointing to the overflowing bags of clothes we've piled into the bed of his truck.

"You? Kenzie Sullivan almost forgot a hockey game?" Damian says.

"There's got to be something wrong with her," Porter says, pressing his palm to my forehead. I push him away.

"Oh, you three. I'll be there. I've just had a lot going on."

"We're playing the IceHoles tonight. You better not ditch out on us." Ty shakes his head as if I've already disappointed him. "Even if you're supposed to 'work' at Trey's."

"Shut up," I say, punching his shoulder.

"Yeah, I'm waiting for you and that one girl on their team to get into a fight. She's such a–" Porter cut his words before saying anything else.

I shake my head. "No fighting. I'd rather play than get ejected."

I take off my gloves, ready to be done for the day. With my brothers' help, it's like a ray of hope that I won't be trying to get through this junk before reaching retirement age.

It's time to get ready for my adult league game. The only hockey I have left.

30

TREY

"How do I get over her?"

This is the last place I thought I'd be tonight. I'm sitting in a bar, trying to help Owen, who's had way too many drinks to get anywhere by himself tonight. At least he'd been coherent enough to call me.

"I'm not sure, O. I think you'll have to find the things you've always wanted to do and do them. And call me when you're having a tough time. You and Riley were together for a long time. It's only natural to feel like this."

He sniffs and I glance down the length of the bar, hoping to find a napkin or a tissue of some kind. The bartender must've read my mind because he slides a napkin in front of Owen.

"Must be a bad one, huh?" the guy says, looking at me but gesturing to Owen.

"Long-time girlfriend left."

The guy looks sympathetic, meanwhile Owen has slumped over the bar and might be snoring.

I pat Owen on the back and say, "Come on, buddy. Let's get you home." We're about the same height which is good so I can sling his arm around my neck and help him at least move forward.

"I'm sorry, Trey. I shouldn't have done this." He sounds like a child trying to apologize.

"It's fine. I've got my car in the parking lot out back and we'll head to your place." The good thing is he hadn't chosen a bar in the heart of the city, where parking would've been difficult to find at a close radius.

When Owen is seated, I get in and start the car.

"How's the datessssss?" Owen asks.

I laugh at the emphasis on the 's'. "Two down, two to go." It's the only thing I can say before thoughts of Kenzie invade. I'm grinning and I can't really help it.

"Your words don't make your expression," Owen says, turning his head toward me while still leaning back against the headrest.

"I think you mean 'match', Owen. And even drunk, you're very perceptive."

"Spill." He leans over and tries to touch the buttons for the radio, but I have to push him back. I don't need Drunk Owen to decide on the station.

Where do I begin?

"Well, the first date I ended up in the pond where the swan boats go, with Kenzie. So that was wet." And really fun. "Then the second date was earlier today. We went to the aquarium."

"You and Kenzie?" Owen asks. The guy barely has his eyelids open and he's firing off these questions. No wonder he makes such a good nurse.

"No, Kenzie and I have not dated. She just doubled with me on the first date."

He grins. "But you want to date her?"

I shake my head, trying not to smile too wide. "I'd be open for a date. I've got two more dates to get through first."

"You sound like that's a bad thing."

"Well, I was so distracted during the date this morning that I barely interacted with my date. She was super nice and we had a lot in common, but I feel bad that I didn't focus on her and give her more of a chance."

"So, call it off. Be done with the matchmaking."

I flip the turn signal and turn onto Owen's street. "We signed a contract. I have to finish."

"Well, make things interesting. If you're going on dates, you might as well have some fun with it."

I think back over the dates we've had so far. They've been tame, with the boat ride and a walk through the museum. Kind of boring, to be honest. Sure, they're great ideas every once in a while, but I need a bit of adventure and some spontaneity.

"That's a great idea, Owen. I'll have to mix it up on the next date."

I drop him off at his house and sit in the driver's seat for a minute, reflecting on the day. It's been a long one, but more mentally than physically. I'm used to it being the opposite.

My phone screen shows a notification from Kenzie and I end up dropping my phone as I try and pick it up from my console. Once I pick it up, I open the message.

Kenzie: Recap sounds great, but my brother is bringing his truck over to my dad's place to haul some stuff for me.

2 hours later

Kenzie: How was your date?

Kenzie: What time was your date?

1 hour ago

Kenzie: Did you fall into one of the tanks and get maimed by one of the sharks?

I'm laughing so hard at her words. The casual questions that escalate to injuries and blood so quickly.

Me: It was around noon. It was good.

Me: Sorry, I had to go rescue Owen from a minor bender.

I put my phone down and start driving, ready to shower and

then fall into bed and sleep. There's some light traffic that makes the drive slower than I want it to be, but I make it home to see another text from Kenzie.

Kenzie: It's good to know you survived the fish. Hopefully Owen is okay.

Kenzie: Who's Owen again?

That gets me laughing even harder. Once I settle down, I call her.

"Hey," she says.

"Hey yourself. What are you doing right now?"

"Great question. I'm heading home from my dad's right now. I'm going to take a shower and then get to bed." There's a pause and then she says, "Did any of the shelving units come yet?"

Straight to business. A twinge of doubt hits me. Does she only converse with me because I hired her?

"I haven't seen any. I'll make sure to check tomorrow morning."

"Okay, like, once they're in, we can put them together and start, like, organizing your life." Kenzie says the end in a strange accent, as if she's become a Valley girl suddenly.

I scan the boxes in the garage and groan. Are we going to have to go through all these? "Maybe you should come over tomorrow and we could get started."

"Putting together invisible shelves?" Kenzie asks with a laugh.

"No, I mean, going through the boxes. Our next date isn't for two days so we've got time. I'm sure there's a bunch of stuff in them that we can organize before we have shelves. I don't want to keep everything forever." But going through them together might be enough time to figure out what she's feeling, if anything toward me.

There's a long pause and I open my mouth to speak, except

she starts talking again. It sounds like she's snacking on something.

"—Could do that. It will be a nice break from garbage and mold."

"Okay, see you tomorrow."

"I can't wait to see what little Trey drew for his class assignments," Kenzie says, giggling.

I grin and say, "Well, you'll be disappointed. It was either something to do with a rocket or hockey stuff."

"Maybe we can submit some of it to the Museum of Fine Art. I mean, I feel like an expert after walking through there for two hours today."

"Not going to happen."

"See you tomorrow." Kenzie hangs up and I'm wondering if there's a way to speed up the docuseries timeline.

31

KENZIE

I'm up early and heading over to Trey's. This could either be a good thing or a complete disaster. The last time I did the walk-through, he was only partially dressed and using a large blanket to cover up, which makes me laugh now thinking back on it.

Armed with a large jug of water and a few high protein snacks, I think I'll survive whatever comes today.

I've got a key, but it feels weird just walking inside and making myself at home. So, I knock.

"Come in," Trey's voice says, startling me.

I open the door and am surprised that the living room floor is covered by totes. Trey walks in from the guest bedroom, carrying one more.

"What's all this?" I ask, waving to the totes.

"I figured I'd get us started. It will probably be easier and more comfortable to look through most of these while seated on the couch. We can turn on a movie at the same time or do whatever." Trey grins and I can't help but match it. He was planning for this to happen.

Sitting on the couch, I drop my bag and my water next to it

and open the first tote. Inside are several small trophies and lots of medals. I pull out a few of them, given to him for the best slapshot or taking second place in a tournament ten years ago.

"You should have these displayed," I say, pointing to the tangle of medals and ribbon. "We could get a shadow box for the medals and then a glass cabinet to display all the trophies."

"You don't think that would be weird? I mean, I've had these trophies for a long time."

I shake my head. "But you earned them. It doesn't matter how long you've had them." Reaching over to my bag, I pull out my notebook.

"What are you writing?"

"I figured we might as well take notes of the things we need to order and our ideas with them. I mean, you've got at least a couple hundred totes. It's going to be hard to remember it all first hand." I glance around. "You don't have any packing tape, or any tape and a Sharpie, do you?"

He comes back with some neon yellow duct tape. "This is all I have. Payton must've left it here after she helped Piper with a school project."

"Do you get along well with your sisters?" I ask, tearing off a piece of the tape. With it stuck to the lid of the tote, I write a large #1 on it and drag it to the side of the room.

"For the most part," he says, chuckling. "They each have very distinct personalities and I'm either mad or rolling on the floor with laughter when they're around. What about you?"

I nod. "I only have brothers, but we all get along. My mom had all three of them with her first husband and thought she was done. So, when she married my dad, I was a surprise. There were a lot of times when my brothers were the babysitters, because they were in high school when I was just starting elementary."

Trey smiles. "I'm sure there are a lot of memories that go with it."

Laughing, I say, "That's for sure. They would just take me along on whatever activity they were doing with friends. They took me rock climbing, with actual hooks and ropes into a mountainside, when I was six. I was terrified at first, but finally got the hang of it."

Opening another box, I pull out what looks like random cards from over the years. There are birthday cards from even his first birthday in here, congratulations for his elementary graduation and so many more. "What do you want to do with the cards?"

Trey frowns. "Um, what do normal people do with cards?"

"Well, if you were my grandmother, she kept them until the day she died tucked in a box like this. But if you don't care about the Hallmark card you got from your aunt's cousin twice-removed, I'd say we could chuck them."

He breathes out a sigh and nods. "Do that then."

He's pulling out several squares of fabric. "What was she going to do with these?"

On the front is the logo of his youth hockey team name. I lean over and see several more pieces. "It looks like your mom was keeping them to make into a blanket. That's really cool. So many memories in one blanket."

"Do you have one?" he asks, putting the squares back in the box.

"No, I've just seen advertisements of people who've turned them into a large quilt. It's a great idea and then you can save some of the things that don't fit anymore."

I turn my attention back to the tote I'm going through, and I realize I need a garbage bag. I stand and go get the box of bags from the kitchen. Between my dad's place and here, the amount of garbage bags I'm using is insane. But all part of the job.

I thumb through each stack of cards I pull out of the box, making sure I'm just throwing away the cards. Halfway through the box, I pause, seeing something very familiar. I pick it up and can barely breathe as I look at my own handwriting from years ago.

As a girl who didn't know how to talk to a guy, I figured the best way to express my feelings was through an anonymous letter.

I opened it, cringing at the wording.

Trey,

You are the best. Thanks for being such a nice person and a great hockey player. I think you'll go far in hockey and I can't wait to watch you on TV. Good luck at school this year. Make sure to come back to hockey camp next year.

Sincerely,

Anonymous

I slap my forehead. I'd written this the first year I'd gone to the camp, at the age of twelve, I think.

Bending over, I see another card with my handwriting on it. I'm not sure I can handle the embarrassment. But then again, he'd kept every card I'd sent him throughout the summer hockey camps, the ones I left near his gear so he wouldn't know I'd delivered them.

"What do you have there?" Trey asks. He scoots over and takes one of the papers from my hand. I thought about fighting him for it, making sure he didn't see it, but then he'd be suspicious.

"Some secret admirer?" I say, trying to act casually.

I watch as his eyes read over the page. He smiles and nods. "Yeah, I got these every year at hockey camp."

"Do you know who they were from?" My lungs are squeezing together as I wait for the answer, making it hard to breathe.

Trey nods and my stomach sinks. "There was a girl named Mac. She was fun and was always watching me when we were on the ice. I'd like to think I taught her how to skate just from her observations." He laughs and hands the paper back. "Keep those."

Frowning, I say, "Keep these? What do you want to do with them?"

"I'm not sure yet. There are a bunch of notes I've gotten from fans over the years. Maybe we can compile them into a book of sorts."

Even though I shouldn't ask the question burning my tongue right now, I need to know. "How did you know this was from the girl at hockey camp?" I ask, waving the note in front of his face.

"I remember seeing her handwriting and it looking just like this. I think she had a crush on me and I didn't want to hurt her. Hockey took a lot of time and I wasn't focused on relationships or anything at the time. She was a great listener, though. Especially when I was trying to decide if I should keep going or not."

The fact that he didn't want to hurt the younger me but also didn't focus on relationships makes me feel a bit better.

"Did you ever go to hockey camps in the area?" Trey asks. His question throws me off guard and I suck in a breath, trying to come up with an answer that won't link me to the girl from the notes.

"I did a few, yeah."

He pulls out a new tote and looks in there. "Every book I had from college is in here. Let's donate it."

"Put it over there on the wall. We'll have a donate pile, a trash pile, and a keep pile."

We work for a few hours, getting through most of the boxes in the room. I sit back on the couch, sinking into the cushions.

"How long have you had this couch?" I ask, laughing as it's basically swallowing me hole.

"About six years. We bought it at a yard sale when we needed one for a new apartment my buddies and I were moving into."

"I hate to say it, but it's got to go."

Trey reaches over and pulls me out of the couch. I end up in his lap, with my face an inch from his. We sit there for a few moments and I keep looking down at his lips. What would it be like to kiss him?

My brain starts whirring, coaxing me to give it a whirl. Carpe diem and all that.

Just as I start to move in, my whole body buzzing with the possibility, a loud knock sends me jumping back and I end up sliding onto the floor.

"Are you alright?" Trey asks, reaching out to help me up.

"Uh, yeah. Totally fine." Except I almost ruined everything by getting greedy and trying to kiss him.

Trey walks over and opens the door. In walk Jack and Spencer.

Jack's gaze searches the room and then he locks on me. "Kenzie, I didn't know you were here."

I wave to the dozens of totes. "Just doing my job," I say.

"Good luck with that," Spencer says, walking over and sitting on the couch, sinking into the hole. "I always forget that's there. You need a new couch, bro."

"I know," Trey says, hovering a few feet away. "We're going to get a new one as soon as we have time to go to the store."

"We?" Jack asks, glancing between Trey and me. "Are you still having trouble making decisions? Please tell me he's not asking to take his mom furniture shopping with you."

Shaking my head, I say, "No, there was no mention of Mama Hatch when shopping."

"Good. Our boy needs to pick out his own furniture and make up his own mind about things."

"Whatever, Jack. What brings you two by in the middle of the day?"

Jack frowns. "Dude, it's six in the evening." He holds out his watch for inspection.

I grab my bag and water bottle. "I'm going to head home. Bye."

Yeah, it was cowardly, but I don't want to be scrutinized by Jack and Spencer in Trey's home. And I'm going to need some time to analyze what in the heck happened between us.

Was it only in my imagination, or had Trey leaned in to kiss me too?

We've still got dates to go on for Love, Austen and this is turning into a giant mess.

Chances are high I'll be the one left with a broken heart.

32

TREY

And the chicken award goes to Trey Hatch. Okay, I'm not a chicken completely since Jack and Spencer ruined what might've been our first kiss. I'm thinking Kenzie might have gone for it because she was leaning.

I just need to tell her how I feel. But how? I've never done something like that before.

It's been twenty-four hours and I'm still getting texts from Jack teasing me about the whole thing.

Me: Are you ready for date #3?

Kenzie: Barely. I'm exhausted, but I managed to get the living room cleaned up at my dad's. So close.

Me: The shelves came this morning. We'll have to put those together tomorrow.

I just need to come up with a good explanation of how to tell her I like her by the time she comes back.

Kenzie: Sounds good. Where is your date tonight?

Me: It says meet in Boston Common.

Kenzie: Are they trying to recreate the swan boats? They need something more original.

Me: Yeah, something more exciting.

It doesn't take long to get to the park in the middle of Boston, but for once, this date is when the sun is going down.

I see the group of camera men. It's like they've tripled from the past couple dates.

"What's going on?" I ask Samantha, who's standing next to the table and going over something with another man on the crew.

"We are getting ready for the dates, of course."

"What is the date, exactly?" I ask, not liking her tone.

Samantha shakes her head. "You'll have to wait and see. Since you're here early, why don't we get you over here for an interim interview?"

I stare at the camera and shake my head. "Not today. I need preparation time to do that."

"Do what?" Kenzie asks. She's next to me and looking between Samantha and me.

"Do another interview. We never redid your first one, Kenzie."

Kenzie shakes her head. "Just do the final one. I'm ready to get the show on the road."

She's got her hair down and curled, a touch of makeup on her face. I've liked her for several days now and she just keeps worming her way deeper into my heart.

Several others show up, the ones I recognize from our first day at Love, Austen.

"Now that we're all here," Samantha says, getting everyone's attention, "we'll get started. Today's date will be a traveling dinner. You'll be able to start with drinks, then move to get appetizers. Another restaurant for the main entrée and then finally dessert. Your dates will be coming in just a few minutes and we'll let you know where to start."

Kenzie turns to me with a thoughtful expression. "I don't know about you but this actually sounds fun."

"Yeah. I've never thought to try different places for a meal.

Who's your date of the night?" I ask, already irritated with the guy.

"Kurt. No, that was the last guy. This one is Sam. Loves hiking and trying different food."

"Sounds fitting for this date. Mine is Liz and she likes to watch sports and play games."

Kenzie frowns. "That sounds weird put together."

I shrug. "I don't write them."

Minutes tick by and we meet our dates.

One of the camera crew comes over to the group and says, "Okay, we'll start with the first four couples at the bar at this address. Everything will be within walking distance. The last four couples will go to this address," he says, handing out pieces of paper to the daters.

"Looks like we're in the second group," I say, holding out a fist to Kenzie. She smiles and bumps her fist into mine.

"You two know each other?" Liz asks, pointing between me and Kenzie.

"Yeah, her roommate married one of my good friends. She's also helping me organize my house. Probably the best one for the job," I say, giving Kenzie a wide grin. Her cheeks flush and she looks away.

"Good to know," Liz says. "I'm excited to get to know you, Trey. I got tickets for your last game this season and it was such a heartbreaker."

All I can do is nod. I don't want to keep reliving the moments of losing this year, which is why I'm kind of itching for the season to start again.

"Thanks for the support," I say. We start walking away from the Common and down one of the side streets. One guy ahead is leading us with his phone map.

"What kind of food do you like?" Kenzie asks her date.

"I like to try stuff that most people cringe at," Sam says. "I don't always like it, but sometimes it surprises ya."

"Cool." Kenzie nods her head and then says, "Are you into any big franchises? Star Wars? Lord of the Rings?" It takes everything inside me to keep from laughing.

"Indiana Jones is more my style."

Kenzie tilts her head, as if studying the guy. "Really? That's one of my favorites."

The two of them continue talking and I'm trying to keep up the conversation with Liz while pushing back the niggling feeling that Kenzie just found a match. Why didn't I say anything yesterday? I could've pretended to not be at home and waited until Jack and Spencer left.

"You don't like the food?" Liz asks, gesturing to my plate once we've made it to the entrée section of the date. "I've never been to Top Shelf and this is probably the best salmon I've ever tasted."

"It is good, huh," I say, taking a bite of my steak. I've been to the restaurant before because my teammate, Carson, owns it. But I'm only focused on the constant chatter between Sam and Kenzie.

"I need to just buy a pass to the paintball place," Kenzie says. "I took my old roommate there to let off some steam after her fiancé broke up with her. Such a good time."

Why is she never this free with words and stories when I'm the target of conversation?

"What are some of your other hobbies?" Sam asks. I'm holding my fork too tight and it starts to bend.

"Hockey is one of my main activities. I love skating out on the ice."

"You'll have to teach me how to skate," Sam says. Over my dead body.

Kenzie shakes her head. "I'm not the best one to learn from. My dad is an excellent teacher. I'll get the two of you in contact and you'll be sailing across the ice in no time."

I want to pull Kenzie into a hug for that move. And then I

remember I'm still on a date. My mother would kill me for being such an airhead.

"Liz, what are some of your favorite things to do?" Why do I hate the small-talk, getting-to-know-the-person conversations that always come on a first date?

"I work at a test kitchen, so I love to enjoy new foods. I'm always trying to analyze how they make certain dishes."

I point toward her salmon. "Did they do anything special with this?"

She shakes her head. "There's nothing out of the ordinary with the salmon but the dill sauce is fantastic. I've never had one with such a pop of flavor before. What about your steak?"

"Um, it's cooked?" I say, and then try to backpedal. "I mean, there are some great flavors there and it was cooked how I like it."

We finish the meal and head out for the final destination.

"It's kind of weird to leave a restaurant and not pay for anything," Kenzie says quietly as we walk out.

We're guided up a couple blocks to a food truck that's parked next to several small tables and a bench.

"Roll With It," Liz reads on the truck. "That's a clever name, especially if they sell rolls and pastries. And it's a food truck."

I laugh and nod, understanding what she's talking about.

A petite woman takes our orders and passes them off to a taller guy behind her. "Thanks for coming to support our food truck. Good luck with your matches, everyone. Brennen and I were matched through Love, Austen and it's worth it." She points to the guy working the machines and grins at us.

"At least some people get the right match," Kenzie says barely audible. She gets her croissant and takes a bite, moaning at how good it is.

"You really like that, huh?" Sam says, pointing to the pastry.

"I just really like chocolate. It always helps calm me down in stressful situations."

Sam frowns. "Is this stressful?"

"Kind of. I mean, there's so much behind these dates. Actual science or just computer systems that are telling us we'd make a good match. It's just... a lot."

"I thought we were having fun."

Kenzie's expression falls and she says, "Yeah, this has been fun. Something different. Sorry, I'm just saying this croissant hits the spot."

There's a tension between them now and I have to turn away to hide my smile.

"How's your dessert?" I ask Liz, trying to stay present.

"It's delicious. A blend of a couple different chocolates and the chocolate ganache is excellent. I'd love to recreate this in the test kitchen."

"Do you have to make everything several times in order to get it right?"

Liz nods, reaching over and placing her hand on my arm. "Yes, once I had to remake the same cake twenty-five times before I got all the measurements right."

"That's a lot of cake."

The camera crews direct us back toward the Common and we say goodbye to our dates. Liz slips me a piece of a napkin with her phone number on it and I have to force a smile when I say we'll have to catch up another time.

"Do you want a ride home?" I ask, turning to Kenzie.

"That would be great. I'm ready to fall asleep standing here."

"How did your date go?"

She lets out a long, slow breath. "To be honest, it was going well for most of the date. And then he got all defensive when I was trying to tell him how I felt about everything. That was a turnoff right there. I don't need to feel like I have to walk on eggshells around him. I've done enough of that to last a lifetime."

"With your ex, you mean?" I ask, curious. She's shared bits about him before, but this is another piece of the puzzle I'd like to hear about.

Kenzie nods. "Oh man, at the time, I was devastated that he'd left me for royalty. But as the months have gone on, I've realized how many red flags there were that I'd conveniently ignored. I gave up so much to be with him and I shouldn't have to change my personality for anyone."

I give her a small smile. "That's definitely the truth. The world needs this Kenzie."

I pull up outside her house, surprised that there's nothing crazy strewn all over the lawn. "Did the prank war end?" I ask.

With a shake of the head, Kenzie says, "No, word is there's going to be a new nurse helping the guy next door. Maybe Mr. Richins has to train them to do that kind of stuff."

"Maybe Owen will know the new nurse. Bookshelves tomorrow?" I ask as she's getting out of the car.

"How about we get the furniture ordered first? Then no one will be lost to the giant hole in your sofa."

"That's a good idea. Then you won't be surprised when you're knee-deep in my childhood artwork and participation trophies."

"You got participation trophies?" she says, laughing. "All I saw were medals and awards for being in the top three, usually first place."

I laugh too. "I know it's hard to believe that someone like me doesn't excel in every aspect of life, but as you might've already put together, I'm lacking in several areas. My mom put me into a square-dancing club when I was ten and I was the only one not given 'Most Improved' or 'Twirling Bird'."

"I'm sorry, but picturing you in a square-dancing club is not something I would've imagined."

"I told you my mom is a bit controlling. Very loving, but good at directing my life. She wanted me to be well-rounded.

Piano, art classes, all of it. Some of them I barely squeaked by with the participation certificates."

"You know how to play the piano?"

"Kenzie, I only know where middle C is. Other than that, musical notes might as well be pictographs." I laugh and say, "Do you want me to pick you up at nine tomorrow? We can hit the furniture store when it first opens."

"Sounds great. Good night." She walks into the house, and I sit there for a few more minutes, trying to configure all the pieces and feelings I have for Kenzie. The woman is amazing and stronger than I took her for. I just wish the last date was out of the way so we could go on our "fun" date.

33

KENZIE

Trey is acting weird the next morning. He's had an iron grip on the steering wheel since I got in with a box of pastries. Hillary had brought them home from a birthday party she'd gone to and he's barely said a word.

"Did you get another concussion? Do I need to drive?" I ask, trying to make him smile.

He shakes his head, like he's a million miles away. "No, I'm good."

"Are you sure? You're acting as though we're driving to Mordor." I crack a smile and he turns to grin at me.

"So, you're not a total hater of the fantasy series."

I shrug. "I've seen them a few times. My brother Damian is an avid fan."

Trey pulls into the parking lot of the closest furniture store. "Are you ready?"

"Are *you* ready?" I ask, laughing. "What is it you'd like to look at?"

He frowns. "All of it?"

Blowing out a breath I say, "You can take me home then. I'm

not going to sit in every recliner and lay on every bed in the place."

His eyebrows cinch together and he says, "But how are we going to know if it's the right one?"

"Okay, we'll narrow it down. I'll allow us to try out three of each." I shake my head. "That makes me sound like I'm your mother. Maybe we should just go with what you want." The guy already has a hard enough time choosing things, he doesn't need me to be controlling on top of it.

He grins, and I'm pretty sure I could stare at that face for the rest of forever.

We walk in and are swarmed by people who work there, wanting to show us to the different pieces of furniture. Working on commission must be the worst thing in the world. Oh wait, that's basically what I'm trying to do. At least I don't have to compete with people to get paid for the same job.

"What kind of vibe are you going for in your front room?" I ask as we walk over to the couches.

"Comfortable." Trey nods, looking over the large selection. He turns to me with another smile and slowly sits down on the first couch. He tries to look casual, but ends up having to move several times to get comfortable.

"I'm going to take that as a no on this one," I say, laughing.

Trey stands up and nods. "Yeah, that definitely doesn't meet the comfortable quota."

Thirty minutes later, he's tried just about every couch in the place. I've even relented and sat on a few.

"Which one's your favorite?" he asks, standing close to me.

I shake my head and say, "It doesn't matter which one I like."

Trey frowns and says, "Throw me a puck here. If it was your house, which one would you pick?"

I raise my arm and point to a large sectional with built-in recliners. It's a rustic blue color and so comfortable.

With a nod, Trey says, "I was thinking the same thing. I think it will fit really well in front of the TV."

"Yeah, and you won't have to worry about sinking through to the bottom." I laugh at the look of surprise on his face.

"Touché." He glances around and says, "Okay, on to the beds."

I swallow hard, surprised by his comment. No words come out and I end up following him in that direction. Beds are an intimate thing, one I don't need to try out while in this store. That would be like waving goodbye to my heart as it fell over the love cliff.

Trey jumps onto just about every mattress in the store, moving back and forth to test them out. I can't help but laugh as he looks almost like a fish out of water.

He pats the space next to him on the fifth mattress he's tried. "Try this one. It's my favorite so far."

I hesitate, not sure I'm willing to kiss my heart goodbye as I imagine a future with Trey. The bed is king size, so I walk to the other side and slide on the very edge, bouncing a couple of times.

"Lay down. You're not going to get the full effect by sitting." Trey reaches over and gently pulls me back.

I settle in and sigh. Wow, this is a really comfortable bed. Better than the one I've been hauling around to my apartments and other places for years. I close my eyes, letting all the tension seep out through my shoulders.

"What do you think?"

I open my eyes and turn to see Trey on his side, propping his head up with his arm. He's so good looking that I have to turn to stare up at the rafters to avoid his gorgeous eyes. "I think this one is pretty much perfect."

"That's what I was thinking," he says, chuckling a bit.

"Look at you making big decisions," I say, smiling as I turn to look at him again. The whole situation is so surreal I might need to start pinching myself. Instead, I sit up and stand, trying to get rid of the strange sensations as I glance around the room. "Is there anything else you want to look at before we leave?"

Forty minutes later we're walking out of the store. The final purchase of all the furniture has lots of numbers after a comma, but we've secured enough pieces for most of the house. At least they'll deliver, because trying to get anything into Trey's car would be laughable.

"Where to next?" Trey asks. "Should we go get some dinner?"

My stomach has been growling for the past fifteen minutes or so and even though I've been trying to stand as the last guard securing the wall around my heart, my resolve is slowly giving in.

"How about the hardware store?" I say, thinking about the shelving units we'll need in his garage. Unless he's ready to get rid of seventy-five percent of the totes in his spare bedroom, we're going to need them.

"I'm not a beaver, Kenzie. I need food, not logs." He tries to keep his face neutral but a grin sneaks in and I can't help but laugh.

"I understand, Trey. Let's go get a few tools to put everything together and then we'll get some food."

He looks at me as we get into the car. "Chinese?"

I shake my head. "I love Chinese, but I'm thinking something else would be good. Tacos?"

His eyes light up and he nods. "I know the perfect place for that."

And I'm a gonner. I might as well organize my own funeral now because there's no coming back from spending time with this guy, even if I never make it out of the friend zone.

34

TREY

I don't know why, but having take-out at my house with Kenzie makes things feel almost perfect. Sure, there's a whole lot of tension between us, but at some point, we've got to address it.

"These are so good," Kenzie says. She takes a bite of her taco and her eyes close as she chews. "I can't believe I've never tried these before."

"They only opened about six months ago. And since they're so close to my house, it's easy to run out and grab them. Do you want to watch a movie?" I ask. Even if she's planning on getting work done while she's here, I don't want to start now.

She looks at the small DVD collection I have from my college days and says, "Sure. I picked last time. What do you want to watch?"

I grin. "Star Wars."

"No."

"Lord of the Rings?"

"No. And no to Star Trek. If you want to do a Harry Potter marathon, I'm in. I can also do the first two movies of the Hunger Games."

Nodding, I say, "How about Indiana Jones?"

Her eyes light up and she says, "Absolutely."

We finish up our food and settle onto the two spots on the couch that aren't a sinkhole. "What is it about Indiana Jones that you like so much?"

"They were my dad's favorite movies. I'd spend weekends after a hockey tournament falling asleep to the adventures of Indy."

"I thought you were going to say you had a crush on Harrison Ford or something."

She laughs and shakes her head. "Naw, he was a lot like my dad."

I find the first movie on one of my streaming services and then we settle in. Kenzie sits up and glances around the room. "Where is your not-so-wholly blanket?"

"The one I wore when you first came over?" We both laugh as I remember that. "It's on the bed."

She disappears into my room and comes out a minute later, tugging the soft ivory blanket and settling in beside me again. Minutes tick by and I feel like a teenager again, unsure of what I should be doing with limbs and if one of her movements should be seen as an opening to some handholding or something.

I finally get my arm up over the back of the couch, feeling like I've just scored the most important goal of my life, when I see her wavering back and forth. Her head droops forward and I can hear a soft snore coming from her.

"Kenzie?" I say softly. There's no snarky answer or smile. And then she leans over so that her head is resting on my upper chest. I freeze, not wanting to ruin this moment.

Seconds tick by and I'm not even sure what's happening in the movie because I'm so focused on the woman who smells like honey today and has slowly been capturing my heart. She doesn't move, only breathes in deeply and snuggles in closer. I wrap my arm around her back, pulling her closer to me. I don't know what took me so long to figure out that I seriously like this woman, but every moment up to this has made it all worth it.

I'm okay that no work has been done tonight. This is exactly where I want to be.

35

TREY

A loud buzzing sound causes me to wake up. The TV is turned off, which means we've been asleep for a while. Kenzie stirs next to me. It's not until she sees my face that her eyes open wider. Her gaze drops to the lack of distance between us and she looks confused.

"Did I fall asleep on you?" she asks. "Eww, I think I slobbered here a bit." She wipes at a spot on my shirt and I laugh.

"It's all good. I think we were both tired. It's been a crazy few weeks."

The buzzing starts up again and Kenzie answers her phone. "What's up?"

She stands up and I can't hear what they're saying on the other end. "Oh crap. Tonight? No, I'm not going to forget every game this season. There's no way we won against the Iceholes in the last game without me."

It's hard to keep a smile off my face with a hockey team name like that.

"Okay, I'll hurry and get there. Did the schedule change or something? I'll text you the address."

She hangs up the phone and starts letting her thumbs fly across the screen.

"Hey, what's wrong?" I ask, walking closer to her.

Kenzie shakes her head and finishes the text. "Nothing. I just forgot about my hockey game and my brothers are never going to let me live it down. We're already short as it is. Damian is coming to pick me up."

"I can drive you wherever you need," I say, lifting my hand to rest on her upper arm.

She gives me a close lip smile and says, "Thanks, but if you're as tired as I am, you might want to stay and relax."

"What about your gear? How are you going to get that?"

With her bag in hand, she says, "My dad keeps it in the back room. Then I don't get complaints from roommates that my stuff stinks."

"Can I come watch?" Why am I pushing so hard?

Something flickers in her eyes and I'm not quite sure what it is. "If you want, sure."

I grab the keys to the car and head to the garage.

For some reason I didn't register the fact that she actually plays hockey. I remember a handful of girls at the hockey camps I went to growing up and I'm curious how good she really is. She claims she used to eat, breathe, and sleep hockey. She's either amazing or awful. And the curiosity is killing me.

"You're going to be bored," she says, buckling up.

"No, I won't. Watching beer league is fun."

She shakes her head. "Not as fun as playing it as a career. We're heading to the Alvey Ice Center."

I grin. "I haven't been there in a while. I used to skate there a lot as a kid."

Kenzie doesn't say anything, looking more agitated than I've seen her.

"Are you nervous?" I ask, trying to hold back a smile.

"A little," she says, closing her eyes for a moment. "I know, it's lame to get nervous because this doesn't mean a whole lot, but the nerves usually fuel into energy once I get onto the ice."

I drop her off and look for parking.

The rink is abuzz with people everywhere and I smile. Even this late at night, the ice brings people together.

I walk past the front desk and am surprised by the man standing there taking money for concessions. Once the line has cleared out, I say, "You've been working here for a while, right? I think I remember you from my youth hockey days."

The man has salt and pepper hair, but his face has barely aged in the last ten to fifteen years.

"That I have. How are you, Mr. Hatch?" He reaches out a hand and I shake.

"It's Trey, thanks. My dad is still the owner of the formal name. Remind me your name again," I say, wishing I had a better memory for names.

"I'm Brian. What brings you here tonight, Trey?"

"Oh, um, my, uh, friend is playing. I asked if I could tag along." I pause, connecting all the dots. "You're the one I bring my skates to. I usually drop them off with someone up front but you do an incredible job sharpening my skates. I should've put that together before now."

Brian leans over the counter and whispers, "Good luck. You're going to have everyone in the vicinity wanting a picture or an autograph." He leans back and nods. "I like it when I get your skates. Something about seeing you in a game and knowing I helped just a bit makes me happy."

I laugh and see several people whispering and pointing toward me. "One of the upsides and downsides of the job." I pause a moment and look at the guy in front of me. "I remember at one camp I attended here, you told us to believe in ourselves and what we could do or would do. You stayed an extra hour after the camp was over and let me practice my slap-shot until I got it right."

With a smile, Brian nods. "I knew you had the potential to be one of the pros. Sometimes kids just need that fostering influence outside their family to nudge them on."

How true that was. It was easy to believe I could do certain things because my mother was always boosting me up, but to have someone not connected to the family and not motivated by money tell me something like that, it changed how I saw myself when it came to hockey.

"I've looked back on those moments and that advice almost daily for the past several years. So, thank you."

"Hey, watch it," a female voice says. I turn my head to see a guy on the ground as Kenzie towers over him. I try to keep a smile back as I watch the scene play out. She's dressed in a blue jersey that says, "Pistol Shrimp" and she's fully decked out in hockey gear, only missing her gloves and helmet.

"I was just trying to say hello," the guy says, scrambling to his feet. As the guy's profile comes into view, I don't recognize him.

She shakes her head. "I've known you for a couple hours on a date, a few days ago, and you want to kiss me after showing up unexpectedly? I don't think so, Kurt."

"You weren't returning my calls," Kurt says, sticking his hands in his pockets.

"That doesn't usually mean you should hunt me down for it. How did you know I would be here now?" Kenzie's eyes are on fire and I duck behind a post before she sees me.

"I did some research. When you said you played hockey at one point and that your dad is the manager, it wasn't hard to figure out."

There is no sound and I'm using every bit of energy to keep from peeking around the pole. I'm already in this position. I might as well not make it worse. Her dad is the manager? She's Brian's daughter?

"There's the door," Kenzie says. "Please don't come back.

Thank you for the date, but I don't think things are going to work out."

"But we both love sports and have similar tastes in movies."

I hear a laugh, and can't help but smile when I recognize it's from Kenzie. "That's great and all, and I did have fun on our date, but you just crossed the line. A girl doesn't want to be kissed without permission or in stinky hockey gear."

"So, I still have a chance? Or did you already find someone else?" the guy asks, his tone making me want to grate my teeth together.

"No, you got one strike and blew it. And why do you sound like it's such a surprise? For your information, yes, there is someone. But my chances of it working out are slim to none. I've got to get ready for a game. Goodbye, Kurt."

I don't move until I see the guy dragging his feet like he'd just been sent to timeout. He makes it through the door when I spin around and see Kenzie face-to-face with me.

"Why were you hiding?" she asks, tying a bandana over her hair.

"I, uh, just got done talking to Brian."

Her gaze darts over to the desk and back. "You know my dad?"

That confirms it. "Yeah, I remember him from all the camps I went to here. Did we ever overlap?" I ask, trying to remember that far back. I don't remember a Kenzie among the handful of girls who went to the camps.

"The rink was my home away from home for a long time." She finishes tying her hair back and I don't know why, but this side of her is just another reason why I'm starting to fall for her. She's strong and could put anyone in their place, especially the paparazzi. And she has a passion for something I love.

"We've been hanging out the last several weeks and I don't even know what position you play," I say.

"Wing. My brothers and I play on a team. My dad used to

play with us but he hurt his knee last year." She lowers her voice. "My money is on trying to get through the garbage heap that has been his house."

"Kenzie, we're on the ice," a guy says from behind her. He's not the same body shape as her, but if he grew long hair, they'd probably look identical.

She flips him off and turns back to me. "You don't have to stay."

Laughing I say, "I don't think I can leave now."

"Don't say I didn't warn you." Without a backward glance, she turns and walks away.

"Trey," Brian calls. "Is Kenzie your friend?"

I nod. "Yeah. She's organizing my house and we've been doing this dating docuseries together."

Brian chuckles. "Ah yes, the matchmaking thing. I've heard her rant about that several times. It's a miracle she decided to do it."

"That's true. I've learned a lot about her. I'm curious if she's as good at hockey as she lets on."

Brian laughs and nods. "It's always a spectacle when those four get on the ice. If they're not yelling at each other about something, it wouldn't be a real game, that's for sure. And Kenzie still has a lot of that energy from her college games."

"Aren't you watching the game?" I ask, pointing toward the ice.

He shakes his head. "In a bit. I can already tell you how things are going to go. That display by my daughter with one of her dates means she's out for blood tonight."

I blink a few times. "Do they allow fighting in the adult league now?" I ask with a laugh.

"No, she won't get into a fight, but she'll be on her A-game and pulling out all the stops. Sometimes her brothers find ways to get her all riled up so she'll play better. And since they're playing the Wreckers, it was one of those times they probably stepped in."

I glance toward the door where Kurt disappeared. "Wait? You think they instigated that thing with Kurt?"

Brian smiles. "I wouldn't put it past them."

"But how would they know who he was? I mean, how would they have contacted him? The show hasn't even aired yet."

"My boys are resourceful, if anything." Brian turns and walks behind the counter to the back room. I turn toward the ice, watching as the two teams warm up. Kenzie's team is at the other end, but now that I know she's out there, I keep my eye trained on number eighteen.

The way she cuts through the ice, using the edges to change directions makes me smile. The woman has skills. She was telling the truth when she talked about being into hockey.

I walk over to the stands and take a seat up high enough to see over the glass, trying to avoid the eyes that are staring at me. Sure, this might not be the best place to go unnoticed because these are hockey people, but I would love to have a little more peace.

The game starts and the play is quick for an adult league game. They're up and down the ice in seconds, battling with the puck.

Kenzie gets it and pulls one of the best fake moves I've seen in a while, moving to the one side, pushing the puck through the guy's legs, and then grabbing it to head up the ice. She flicks it to the right side and the puck is caught by the goalie near the upper corner of the goal but I'm not focused on that anymore.

That move reminds me of someone I used to know. It's like déjà vu at this rink. I try to remember what she looked like compared to Kenzie now.

What was her name?

Mal? Mar?

Mac. It was Mac.

And now I'm putting all the pieces together. Mackenzie.

Shame washes over me. That must be why she was so mad at me after my game several weeks ago. I didn't recognize her. I mean, it's hard after more than a decade to remember every face I've ever met, and now that I'm constantly in the public eye, I struggle with names.

I smile, thinking of those summer camps. Mac was a couple years younger than me, but she was always there, trying to learn the moves I was trying out and repeating them. The guys always made fun of her behind her back when we were in the locker room, saying that she had a crush on me. I'd always brush it off and talk about the next thing that would be happening at the camp.

Did Kenzie really have a crush on me back then?

The letters Kenzie found. She'd been so stiff holding them out, wondering if I remembered the girl who wrote them.

Obviously crushes come and go, especially after this long, but now I'm curious about my new friend.

That word sounds wrong. So wrong, like I struck a bad note on a piano.

The attraction I feel toward her, especially seeing her on the ice, taking part in a sport I love, is even higher now than it has been the past week.

Questions circle through my mind as I continue to watch the game. I stay and then wait in the lobby, watching the hallway to the locker rooms.

"Can you tell me one thing?" I ask, as I hand him my card to pay for a bag of popcorn and a box of chocolate candy.

"Sure," Brian says, pushing buttons on the monitor.

"I used to come here for camps when I was younger and there was a girl, Mac I think her name was. Do you know what happened to her?"

Brian's head snaps up and he looks at me before glancing

behind me. I'm not sure what he's looking for, but he finally looks back at me.

"You just watched her play," he says quietly.

"Is it Kenzie?" I ask, leaning forward and trying to keep my voice down. It's not like this is a state secret, but I'd prefer not to experience what Kurt went through an hour and a half ago.

Brian smiles and says, "Yes, but you didn't hear that from me."

"Why did she change her name?" I ask, hoping it will give me some more insight into who she is.

With a long sigh, Brian shakes his head. "I don't know a whole lot about women, as evidenced by the ones that keep leaving me because of my major quirks, but I think she needed a new start. She changed after she started hanging out with Hillary and wanted to start over in college."

I frown, trying to put all the pieces together. I'd met Hillary at the game and at the race, recognizing her as Jack's old friend. But the Mac I knew pairing up with Hillary seemed like a long shot.

"So, were the changes good or bad?"

"Not bad, I mean, she went from having braces and glasses with a face full of acne to the woman we see now. I'd say she just needed time to mature a bit more." Brian smiles and I nod.

"Well, time has been good to her then," I say, turning around.

Kenzie walks down the hall toward us, her long hair wet from a shower. I can't help but smile as I see all the changes in her from over the years. But now I can see the similarities.

"You stayed?" she asks, tucking a section of hair behind her ear as she looks up at me.

"Yeah, I had to see if you had a big ego or if you can really game." I stuff my hands into the pockets of my pants and grin at her.

She raises an eyebrow and says, "And?"

"You've got some moves," I say, trying to decide if I share what I know about her yet.

Her wide grin at my compliment causes me to smile and I don't want that to disappear just yet.

"Thanks for watching."

We both wave to her dad and walk toward the entrance. "It was fun to be the spectator for once. I mean, you got to see me in action. It's only fair I got to see you."

She tosses her head back and laughs. "Let's be honest, I was able to pull out a move every once in a while. It's different playing once a week compared to practicing daily."

"True. I can feel a difference when I haven't practiced in several days."

We walk out to my car. "Do you want to go get something to eat?" I blurt.

"That sounds so good right now, but I need to get home to bed. I mean, I passed out at your house and didn't get anything done. Maybe a full night of rest will help that."

"What do you think will happen tomorrow?" I ask, curious about who her last date would be. I'm more worried about that than I am my own date, and I was the one who wanted to find a partner in the first place. "Maybe you'll find someone who is a Harry Potter or Star Trek fan. Just round out all the fantasy kingdoms."

"Yeah, that's all I need. Don't get me wrong, I might be willing to watch anything my date wants to watch, but I don't need a play-by-play commentary throughout the entire thing."

"Do you think you'll get a good match?"

Kenzie laughs again. "No, I've said the whole time that I think I'm cursed. What about you? Any chances of a relationship happening from this dating torture?" Her smile fades and she focuses on the keys in her hand.

"I don't know. I mean, I know we're supposed to have a lot in common with most of these people, but there are slight differences that are hard to get past."

"Amen to that."

I take a step forward, curious what she'll do.

"What are you doing?" Kenzie asks, searching my face for the answer. I'm stuck on her eyes, surprised by how much I want to keep looking at them.

"Just remembering this moment."

She turns her head to the side, as if she's going to be pranked or something. Then she turns to look at me, and I remember the short history between us from way back when.

"What if we don't show up tomorrow? Maybe we can take a drive up to Maine or something." The words are spilling from my mouth so fast that my brain hasn't had time to catch up.

That has her attention. "You want to ditch out on the final date of filming and your last date? Why?"

There are so many emotions coursing through me right now that I'm not exactly sure what I'm thinking. I have a contract with the matchmaking company, the same people who are trying to help me find someone to settle down with.

But as I stare at Kenzie, I realize that I might've found that person all on my own.

"Well, didn't Meg say something about the matches getting progressively better?"

Kenzie nods. "Yeah, so maybe you'll get your dream, Turbo." I can't miss the frown on her face and the slumping of her shoulders as she says that.

"Why not move the fun date up?"

She gives me a sad look and shakes her head before taking a few steps back. "Did you bump your head? Do I need to call a doctor? What about your happily ever after?"

"No, I haven't hit my head on anything. But there are a few things I realized." I pause a moment, trying to figure out the best way to ask the question burning inside me. "Why did you change your name from Mac to Kenzie?"

Her expression is pure shock. "W-what? Why would you ask that?"

I try to reach out and take her hand but she backs away. "I put a few pieces together. I'm sorry I didn't recognize you at first. Seeing you play brought up all the old memories. Your flick move—"

"I think I forgot something inside," she says, taking several more steps backward. "Don't wait for me. I'll have my brother drop me off."

"Kenz, why are you being weird? I can take you home."

She waves her hand and says, "I'm good. It's okay. Just go."

And then she turns and runs back into the rink, disappearing through the doors.

This is the time when I wonder if I should go after her, if I should tell her that I have feelings for her. But at the beginning of our relationship, she was skittish and would barely talk to me. I don't want to drive her away if all she needs is a bit more time.

I don't know whether to take that as a rejection or as nerves on her part. But there's so much I want to figure out when it comes to her.

My phone rings loud against the stillness of the outside and I answer it when I see Meg's name on the screen. "Hey Meg."

"We'll be filming tomorrow. I've got something to show you. Can you meet me at the office in the morning?"

"You're going to make me wait all night?" I say, wondering what could be so important that she needed to schedule a meeting.

"You're right. Do you have time to swing by the office? Maybe we can come up with a plan."

36

KENZIE

I feel like a teen, with a crush who's just told her he's not interested. Then again, Trey never said anything like that. But it was like he knew that I was Mac long before I admitted anything. Had he remembered?

Well, I've screwed it all up anyway.

My dad tried to talk me out of running, but it's a defense mechanism to protect my heart. It's the least I can do since Trey pulled down all the walls.

I know, it's irrational. Who cares if he knows I was the geeky girl who followed him like a puppy and left him notes?

I do. I might've changed the outside appearance, but the girl inside doesn't feel like much has changed.

Curling up on my bed, I try to take long deep breaths. As much as I'd love to just stay in this room forever, I'm going to have to leave at some point. Trey still needs his house put together and I don't know if I can do that. Should I quit? I can remove myself from that situation and then just keep working at my dad's house. I'll get other jobs, right?

But there's the final date. I'll have to see Trey anyway and then avoid every friend group activity until the end of time.

This is why I should have kept my heart walled off and continued on the path I was taking.

There's a knock on the door and I don't say anything, hoping whoever is outside will go away.

"Kenz?" Evie says, opening the door. "I heard you come home. Are you okay?"

I stare at the ceiling. "I think I'll just become part of the bed here."

Evie limps over, looking like she's in pain. "You can't just sit here. What happened at the game?"

"Why are you limping?" I ask instead, sitting up.

She gives me a small smile before she sits on the edge of the bed. "My leg started hurting a little bit ago. I'm thinking it's just from sitting on it weird for too long. Tell me, what happened?"

"He knows I'm Mac. I don't know how he found out, but it was like he was waiting for me to confess to it."

"Is that such a bad thing? You've been worried about keeping that a secret for so long. Maybe this is good. There are no secrets between you two now. You can keep going forward."

I shake my head. "I can't face him again. Knowing he remembers the chubby girl with acne and glasses. It would be too hard."

Evie laughs. "I seem to remember you taking Rachelle to a paintball arena to get over her breakup with Landon because she needed to do something uncomfortable. And you went into starting your own business with the confidence you can do it. That stuff is hard. I know. So be tough, and face him. Tell him you've liked him for a while."

"But I don't want to get hurt again. Donovan's whole act obliterated me for a long time."

"Did Trey do something similar? Did he look at you like scum because of who you used to be?"

"No."

"Did he drop you off and say, 'See you never!'"

"No. Wow, Evie, you're kind of intense." I laugh, wiping at a stray tear.

"Well, I have to be when I know my friend is about to make a mistake. Don't give up on something so small. I know you've got so many feelings from growing up and trauma responses, but don't let that stand in the way of your future. Go get Trey."

I close my eyes, wishing that was a possibility. "We still have the last date. This one should be the closest to our match that we can get. So, I just blew my chance with him."

"Who knows? Maybe you'll get your fun date after all."

If only that were true.

37

KENZIE

I feel like I got hit by a truck. Sleep evaded me completely and now I just want to fall over and sleep on the ground.

The producer called me to say that we are finishing the date and interviews today. I let Evie and Hillary dress me up, putting on makeup on me, while Millie bounced around trying to figure out who would be my next date.

The info text came in:

Bryce who loves swimming and anything outdoors.

I make it to the Love, Austen office where I have to endure the first interview all over again. At least my lips are a normal size this time.

There are so many questions that my head starts to hurt. Why can't they just ask three questions and call that good? Then again, I tend to clam right up and get sarcastic during these times.

"Okay, Kenzie, you'll meet your date at the Alvey Ice Rink. There's a car outside waiting to take you there." Samantha has already started walking away.

"Where's Trey?" I ask. I don't want to see him but I also don't know what I'd do without him on this date. We've been like partners in crime, wingmen to the random and awkward things that have happened on our dates.

And now he knows that I was the awkward girl who liked him all those years ago.

"He's been assigned to his meeting place already." Maybe it's for the best.

I nod, trying to digest this piece of information. I shouldn't have run away from him last night. But all the insecurities cropped up and I didn't need the pity or the look of rejection from him eventually. Maybe this will be good.

Kenzie: I know you're going on a date soon, but can we talk after?

Kenzie: I'm sorry about last night. I've worked hard to be someone different than the girl I was all those years ago, but there's still a piece of me that worries I'll go right back to that time and mental headspace. Have fun on your date and I hope to see you after.

Taking in a deep breath, I resolve to be open minded on this date. Who knows if Trey won't fall for the woman he's with? This date will probably be closer to a match for him.

The car pulls up to the rink and I try to calm down as I search for Dad's car. It's not here. He's usually working the afternoons for sure.

There are only two other cars in the parking lot, which is strange for this time of day. The ice is always packed with different skating activities and local groups.

The door opens and a man waves me out of the vehicle. "We're filming," he says through clenched teeth. I nod, trying to compose myself in two seconds before stepping out of the car. This almost feels like a *Bachelor* moment and I should be wearing a formal gown and heels. Instead, I'm in a comfy pair of stretchy jeans and a semi-nice t-shirt.

I see crew member waving for me to walk over to the front

door so I start in that direction, trying to avoid the cameras
following me everywhere.

Of all the places I thought we'd go for this date, the ice was
not even on the radar. My hope lifts that maybe the guy I'm
matched with has an interest in skating or hockey. There's no
way I'm giving up all the things I love for a guy, not again.

I'm at the door and I open it, all the emotions crashing
down over me. I've walked into this place nearly a hundred
thousand times and for some reason, this feels different.

I've got the first door open and step inside the breezeway. A
movement catches my eye. My dad runs over to the door and
locks the door behind me.

"What are you doing, Dad?" Where did he park his car?

"I think you need a few private moments for this," he says
with a wink.

Instead of understanding what he's talking about, I frown.
"Please tell me my date is not *that* bad to warrant being locked
in an ice rink. Are we waiting for a police escort to arrest
someone?"

Dad grins and says, "I think you'll be pleasantly surprised."

Behind us, there are cameramen pounding on the door,
pointing their cameras through the glass in an attempt to get
some footage.

"Dad, I'm supposed to be on a date right now. What are you
doing?"

"He's just doing what he's told," a familiar voice says, I turn
to look at the silhouette walking toward us from the dark empty
rink.

Trey walks out, holding a daisy. My heart beat ticks up as if
I'm running a marathon.

"Aren't you supposed to be on a date?" I ask, shifting to the
side as if I'm going to see some model hiding.

"I am," he says, reaching out his hand. I take the flower and my dad waves us through. He hands Trey the keys and says, "I'll see you later, you two."

"What's going on?" I ask, still dumbfounded that my dad has willingly handed over his keyring to Trey when I get stern lectures and badgering if I ask to borrow them.

Trey's grin makes me think that this is all a big joke and I push past him. "Okay, where are the extra cameras?"

He flips on a light and I can see little twinkle lights set up around the lobby and all around the rink. Twinkle lights have always been my favorite thing, the first thing I think of when it's almost Christmas time. There's a little bit of magic in those lights and I'm still trying to put together what's going on.

"Are you on a date with *me*?" I ask, my words barely above a whisper. I just don't want him to contradict them.

Trey nods, looking as happy as he's ever looked. "Yes, Mackenzie Sullivan, I'm on a date with you."

Frowning, I pull out my phone, knowing I must be dreaming. "The note I got for today was that I would meet Bryce, who is an outdoor enthusiast."

Trey laughs and pulls out a folded piece of paper. "I figured you wouldn't believe me, so I had Meg print this off for you."

"Meg? Did you see her or something?"

He nods. "Last night. She called me to talk about, um, a few things for this contract."

The piece of paper is in my hands but I'm worried that whatever is inside, it will change my life for the worse. I count to three in my head and open it up.

The top of the page has the Love, Austen logo displayed and then a bunch of information. A quick glance only has me more confused.

Going back slowly, I see my name at the top with a bunch of other information that I don't understand. I pull back the other third of the page and see several names there. All three of my former dates are there with their percentage of matching with me.

And then there is a name that makes me think I've died and gone to heaven because it says that Treydon Hatch is a 97% match for me.

My insides are having a dance party while I try to keep my composure on the outside.

"What do you think of this?" I ask, my brain going back to the insecurities that began with Donovan. But I shake them off. No matter if Trey is happy or he hates the idea, I don't need to change to be seen.

"I have to say I'm very happy with how this turned out." He's searching my face, waiting for me to respond.

A few moments of silence pass and I say, "You're happy that I'm here?"

"Kenzie, I'm not quite sure when it happened, but being around you the past couple weeks has made me want to be with you all the time. I'm constantly wondering what you would think about random things and wishing you were near me when you're gone. Remember last night when I said we should just blow off the dates and go do something?"

I nod, biting my upper lip in an attempt not to cry.

"It's because I want to be with you Kenzie. I want you to be my girlfriend and to have you there at all my games cheering me on. I want to be at all your games too, to make a go of this and see where it leads."

He pauses and there's no way I can say anything without my voice breaking like I'm going through puberty. I nod, trying to figure out if this is real or not.

"So, taking me shopping for furniture was...?"

"A way to get your opinion on it. I know, I've had a lot of trouble picking out things and looking like an adult when it comes to my house and other decisions, but you've helped me see that it's okay to ask for help when you don't know the answer. And it's okay to like something, even if it's not what other people would do. Thank you for giving me that confidence to make my own decisions. And I'm pretty sure I want your opinion to be the one that matters in my life."

My mind is racing, making it hard to focus on any one thought or emotion for too long.

"But I was the dorky girl who had a crush on you all those years ago," I say, hiding my face in my hands.

His fingers touch my hands, pulling them away. He ducks down and gives me a small smile. "Kenzie, we all have dorky times and what I remember of you was a girl who kept pushing, kept working to get what she wanted. You were the boss out on the ice during those camps and you're basically the boss now, when it comes to organizing my house."

I laugh, shaking my head at that. "You don't remember the braces? The thick glasses and acne?"

Raising an eyebrow, Trey says, "I don't. I was worried about my own acne and the chip on my tooth from falling down the stairs. Or the worry that the guys would laugh at me for not knowing everything they talked about. I was a bit sheltered, as you can imagine."

Everything in his words rings true and I can't help but let a tear slide down my cheek.

"Don't cry, Mac—Kenzie. The last thing I ever want to do is make you cry."

I sniff and take in a deep breath. "It's not a tear of sadness, but of joy."

Trey searches my face for something. Before he can ask another question, I say, "I've dreamed of this moment for way too long. When Dani married Miles, I figured it would be torture to see you all the time. But these past few weeks have been some of the best. Treydon Hatch, it looks like we match." I giggle at the rhyme.

"So, will you be my girlfriend?" he asks, stepping closer and wrapping his arms around my back. Our faces are inches away and this whole thing seems like a dream.

"I would love to be your girlfriend."

Trey leans down and brushes his lips across mine in a quick kiss. I'm about to protest the quickness of it when he kisses me again, only this time, I wrap my arms around his neck and pull closer, not wanting him to move away for even a moment.

Every nerve ending is on fire throughout my body. I've done a lot of daydreaming, pretending I would know what this moment was like if it ever happened to me, but this is far surpassing every expectation. The guy knows how to kiss and I am here for it.

When we finally pull back for air, I lean forward, resting my forehead on his chest.

"Are you okay?" Trey asks, using his pointer finger to gently tilt my chin up.

"More than okay," I say. "I can't believe you did all this for me." I wave to the hundreds of lights and grin.

"Well, your dad helped. I owe him, which means I'll be your assistant when you work at his house."

I laugh and nod. "Sounds just like Dad." There's a banging on the doors and I turn to see the camera crew still locked outside. "Should we let them in?"

Trey leans down and gives me a kiss. "Do we have to?"

"I'm pretty sure they have to film some of this. But once they get everything put together, it should help the matchmaking company out, right? I mean, I was cursed before."

"Not cursed, just waiting for your happily ever after. Or your one day at a time kind of happy?"

I laugh and nod. "I think we both deserve the happily ever after."

EPILOGUE

Kenzie

If someone had asked if I thought I'd be part of a "Where are they now?" episode, I would've laughed hysterically. And yet here I am, checking every bit of the makeup the people are applying to my face so I avoid looking like a blowfish again.

Trey and I have been dating for the past six months and several items have been checked off my lists. We got his house organized and the pictures from it look so good on the website. He also helped me get my dad's house cleaned. Having tickets to every game and being able to cheer him on, even giving him encouragement when he's had a rough game, is a dream come true. He even worked it so I could be the person behind the net who pushes the button when there's a goal. Another bucket list item unlocked.

Dad has been going to therapy for his hoarding problems and aside from a quick cleanup every week when I check in, he's been able to keep things low maintenance and clean. He's even talked about meeting up with Sherry a few times. I hope they get back together. She's always been good for him.

"Can you believe we're here?" Trey says, leaning over to kiss me once the makeup ladies step back.

"No, definitely not. Are there any swelling parts of my face?"

Trey takes a quick look and shakes his head. "I think we're all clear on that front."

Samantha Jordan walks in with her still semi-fake smile. "Okay, we're ready to get started. We have a few questions for the two of you. There will be a video montage of the footage we have of you both. I guess people go for that kind of thing," she says drily.

Trey and I lock eyes for a moment and I know he's thinking the same thing I am. If it wasn't for our relationship with Meg, we would've turned down this offer.

"Action," one of the camera crew says, and I wonder if they got sent to the wrong set. There isn't a whole lot of action here.

"When did you know that you would be matched with Kenzie?" she asks Trey.

"The night before the final date."

A video of the last date comes up and I sit there watching it for a few moments, getting a bit emotional about the whole thing.

"Explain what we just saw," Samantha says. For once she's looking at me.

"Well, I was told my date would meet me at the rink and was surprised to find Trey was my match."

"I take it the two of you are for matchmaking then?"

It's a question we've asked ourselves a few times over the months. Would we have gotten together if we hadn't been forced on so many strange dates and just hung out in the friend groups? I'm not sure I could've broken myself out of the friend zone.

"I do," I say, nodding. Samantha gasps and I turn to see what she's seeing.

Trey is down on one knee. "Can you save that answer for a later date? Like the day you marry me, MacKenzie Sullivan?" He holds out a ring that's simple and just my style.

"Smooth," I say under my breath. The guy was terrified of cameras and here he is proposing with too many of them on us to count.

"We'll laugh until the day we die. We'll have takeout in our comfies and not fall through the couch cushion. Also, I'd say we should avoid any unnecessary swelling of the face. Swimming in a pond is also not ideal. But I'm okay to kiss you and take care of you in all those situations."

The grin on my face probably makes me look like a clown, but this is happiness, pure and simple. Finding joy in the daily life and making our own story.

"I would love to marry you, Treydon Hatch." I pull him up and give him a kiss even Samantha comments on.

In a million years, I didn't think I would be in this position. But sometimes you have to take a chance with your athlete boss.

ALSO BY BRITNEY M. MILLS

Romance by Love, Austen

Matched with Her Runaway Groom

Matched with Her Fake Fiancé

Matched with Her Athlete Boss

Love Austen Series

Love, Austen

Austen, Party of Two

Austen Unscripted

Matched, Austen

Austen, Edited

Testing Love, Austen

International Billionaire Club

The Australian Billionaire

The French Billionaire

The British Billionaire

The Vegas Billionaire

The Italian Billionaire

Christmas at Coldwater Creek

Love in a Blizzard

Love in the Lights

Love in a Snapshot

Love in the Details

Rosemont High Baseball

The Perfect Play

The Perfect Game

The Perfect Catch

The Perfect Steal

The Perfect Hit

Sage Creek Small Town Series

Loving His Flower Shop Girl

Loving His Reporter Girl

Subscribe to the newsletter to get updates on books coming out, cover reveals and the opportunity for giveaways!

ABOUT THE AUTHOR

By day, Britney M. Mills is the wife to a builder and mom to five, but by night, she turns into an author, writing YA & contemporary romance stories.

A book lover, former college athlete, and Jane Austen fan, she crafts stories with the idea that anyone can find love.

When she's not writing, she spends time playing games with her kids, or shuttling them to and from their activities, watching Sanditon and Murdock Mysteries, or dreaming of future characters while she folds a mountain of laundry.

Subscribe to Britney's newsletter for updates, behind-the-scenes and a free book to dive into today!

Made in United States
Troutdale, OR
10/16/2023

13775613R00152